UNEXPECTED
PARTNERS

Visit us at www.boldstrokesbooks.com

By the Author

Mercy

Unexpected Partners

UNEXPECTED PARTNERS

by

Michelle Larkin

2018

UNEXPECTED PARTNERS

ISBN 13: 978-1-63555-203-4

This Trade Paperback Original Is Published By
Bold Strokes Books, Inc.
P.O. Box 249
Valley Falls, NY 12185

First Edition: December 2018

CREDITS
EDITOR: RUTH STERNGLANTZ
PRODUCTION DESIGN: SUSAN RAMUNDO
COVER DESIGN BY TAMMY SEIDICK

Acknowledgments

Boundless gratitude to my editor, Ruth Sternglantz, for her insight, guidance, and keen eye. This story wouldn't be what it is today without her.

Sincere thanks to Tammy Seidick for designing yet another beautiful cover.

Thank you to Sandy Lowe, the book blurb whisperer.

A very special thank you to my dog and dearest friend in life for giving me nine wonderful years. Her recent departure inspired the addition of Taz to this story.

Another special thanks to my mom for her enthusiasm and support…and for helping me see we all have a path that's meant just for us.

And, finally, a huge shout-out to my two sidekicks, Levi and Jett, who fill my world with endless wonder, laughter, and love.

Dedication

For all the loyal Taz's out there who love us flawed humans unconditionally—thank you for leading by example.

CHAPTER ONE

Tantalizing aromas of blended coffee beans and fresh-baked cookies filled the small café. "Absolutely not," Dana Blake said, sipping her coffee.

"But she checks all the boxes." Maribel Murphy had been Dana's friend and sole confidant for the past four years. She was unrelenting in her quest to set Dana up on a blind date.

"And what boxes are those?" Dana glanced over Maribel's shoulder as the door swung open and another customer entered in need of their morning caffeine fix. Boston's chilly November air drifted in and grazed her hand as she set the mug down. She'd selected a table with a view of the door, positioning herself with her back to the wall—a habit she'd developed from her time on the streets as a cop. Even now, as a plainclothes detective, it was a habit she couldn't shake. She had already done her usual Saturday morning assessment of everyone in the café. She was off the clock, but these days you could never be too careful.

"Smart, sexy, athletic, and not a cop." Maribel sipped her own coffee and studied Dana with a scrutinizing gaze. "Or a prosecutor," she added.

"What do I have against prosecutors?"

"Chris Slater," Maribel shot back.

She laughed out loud. "Seriously?"

"Everyone in the office knows he chased after you for years. You rejected him at every turn."

"Not because I have something against prosecutors. I never went out with him because I'm gay."

"I thought you were bi."

Dana frowned. "How on earth did you get that impression?"

"You mentioned a boyfriend in college." Maribel cast her eyes to the floor in thought. "Charlie. That was his name."

"Charlie was a spring fling—"

"So you *were* bi."

"And her full name was Charlene," Dana finished.

"Oh." Maribel leaned back in her chair. "So you really don't have anything against prosecutors?"

She shook her head. "I'd even date you if you batted for my team." As one of the top ADAs in Boston, Maribel was smart, headstrong, independent, and beautiful. Exactly her type.

"I'm flattered. And I'd date you if I liked women. You're totally hot."

"Thanks," Dana replied, genuinely grateful for the compliment. They'd been working cases together for years and had developed a solid friendship that allowed them to speak their minds without fear of judgment. Dana had never been attracted to Maribel. She'd never even thought about it until now. Their chemistry was in the friendship department. Nothing more.

"Will you at least think about meeting her? I invited her over for drinks tonight at seven and told her you'd be there."

She knew Maribel had her best interests at heart, but this was getting old. "I'm not ready."

Maribel softened her gaze and leaned forward. "It's been four years. I miss Gabbi, too. But she'd want you to move on at some point."

Maribel and Gabbi had been best friends for years before Dana entered the picture. Gabbi's death was just as much Maribel's loss as it was hers. She was sure Maribel was right, but she couldn't force herself to open up before she was ready. Closure was all she needed. She could only get that closure by finding the bastard who murdered Gabbi and putting him behind bars.

The door to the café swung open again. Dana recognized this customer at once. A recent addition to the Boston PD, Chloe Maddox was building a solid reputation as a sex crimes behavioral profiler. They hadn't worked a case together yet, but she was sure their paths would cross eventually.

Maribel followed Dana's gaze as Chloe stepped in line. "That's Dr. Maddox. We're working a few cases together. Have you two met?"

She shook her head, still staring. Wearing a red windbreaker, gray leggings, and black and white Hoka sneakers, Chloe was obviously a runner. A red headband covered her ears, and her wavy blond hair was pulled back in a ponytail. With her bagged pastry and coffee to go, she turned and headed toward the door.

"Chloe!" Maribel stood and waved her over.

Chloe looked back, smiled, and walked over to join them. Her cheeks were flushed from cold and exercise.

"I see you've already found the best café in town."

"Chocolate almond croissants." Chloe held up the white paper bag and grinned. "I'm addicted. This is my reward after my run."

Dana couldn't take her eyes off Chloe. She was gorgeous.

Maribel looked back and forth between the two women. "Dana's a runner. Maybe the two of you could run together sometime."

She finally tore her eyes from Chloe to give Maribel a look of warning.

Oblivious to the warning—or, more than likely, choosing to ignore it—Maribel went on, unhindered. "Chloe, this is Detective Dana Blake."

Dana stood and reached out to shake hands.

"I've seen you around the station." Chloe set her coffee on the table and reached back. "Nice to finally meet you."

"You, too," she said, impressed by the firm handshake. Limp introductions irked her to no end. "How do you like it here so far?"

"Not bad. The Vineyard was too quiet. Boston suites me better."

"From what I've heard, we're lucky to have you." Catlike hazel eyes stared back at Dana, making her uncharacteristically nervous.

"Thanks. How many miles?"

She was so taken by Chloe's beauty she couldn't quite comprehend the question. "Huh?"

"How many miles do you run?" Chloe asked.

She cleared her throat and willed her brain to focus on the conversation. "Five, usually."

Chloe smiled. "Same here."

"Then maybe we should go running together sometime." The words were out of her mouth before she realized what she was saying. She could feel Maribel's unbridled enthusiasm from across the table.

"I'd like that." Chloe's eyes lingered on Dana before she turned to Maribel. "We still on for Monday?"

Maribel nodded, barely able to contain the smile that was obviously fighting like hell to break the surface.

Chloe cast her eyes on Dana once again. "Nice to finally meet you." She grabbed her coffee, turned, and swiftly disappeared into the sea of customers.

Dana sat back down and sipped her lukewarm coffee. She could still smell subtle wisps of a sweet fragrance she would now associate with Chloe. "What's on Monday?" she asked, feeling nosier than usual as she turned her attention back to Maribel.

"Court. She's helping with a case." Maribel drained the last of her coffee. "Jealous?"

"Martha's Vineyard has its own police department?"

Maribel nodded. "Four, actually. Chloe was a cop with the Tisbury PD. She went back to school to get her doctorate in psychology with a subspecialty in sex crimes. She's damn good at interviewing victims, getting them to talk when no one else can."

"Why sex crimes?" she wondered aloud.

"I have no idea. Maybe you can ask her yourself when the two of you go running together," Maribel said with a self-satisfied smirk.

"We'll see." Something about Chloe nagged at Dana. Something she couldn't put her finger on.

"I know that look." Maribel rolled her eyes and sighed. "What's wrong now?"

"I don't know. Maybe nothing."

Maribel leaned forward. "Spill it."

She shrugged. "I feel like I've seen her somewhere before."

"Where?"

"I can't remember," Dana admitted, searching her memory banks at warp speed.

"I'd imagine she's kind of hard to forget, especially for someone like you."

"What's that supposed to mean?"

"All I'm saying is she's drop-dead gorgeous. Even for a mere mortal like me, she'd leave a lasting impression. Let's face it, being a lesbian is your secret superpower."

She narrowed her eyes. "How so?"

"It's like you've been inoculated against the influence of well-defined biceps in the male population. In my book, that makes you superhuman."

Dana laughed. She knew Maribel was a sucker for a handsome face and decent biceps. This fiery ADA had a long history of failed relationships with men who could never quite measure up in the intelligence department.

They finished their coffee, hugged, and parted ways, agreeing to meet up for lunch on Tuesday at their favorite burrito cart outside the courthouse. She shoved her hands inside her coat pockets and hurried to her car as fat raindrops pummeled the sidewalk with an audible *splat*.

Hunching her shoulders against the oncoming storm, she found her thoughts returning to Chloe. Where in the world had she seen her before? It was going to drive her crazy until she figured it out.

❖

"Can't get her to talk." Detective Dana Blake sat on the edge of the desk, one hand resting comfortably on the gun at her hip, the other massaging her temple. "Sorry for calling you in so late."

Chloe glanced at the clock on the station wall: two thirty a.m. This wasn't the first time she'd been roused from sleep by a detective, and it wouldn't be the last. As the newly appointed sex crimes behavioral profiler for the Boston PD, she was often called upon to elicit information from a victim who was either too scared or too traumatized to talk.

She set her briefcase down. "Fill me in. What do we have so far?" Chloe studied the detective as she spoke.

A small heart-shaped pendant hung from a thin gold chain and rested between the points of Dana's collarbones. Her formfitting, honey-colored sweater swooped into a low V-neck. The brown crewneck underneath tastefully covered what the sweater did not, effectively drawing attention away from her chest and up to large dark knowing eyes.

Dana was stunning but still somehow managed to be just one of the guys. From afar, Chloe had watched other cops interact with her, and she admired the way Dana handled herself. Forthright, intelligent, and more than capable of handling herself if a physical confrontation arose. The athletic curves of her body, graceful hands, and shoulder-length black hair hinted that something more feminine lurked beneath the hard outer shell of a cop. She moved with purpose and confidence, seemingly unaware of how many eyes followed her in the course of a day.

Chloe wasn't sure what had prompted Dana to make the leap to detective, but she'd heard she was very good at her job. With eight years under her own belt as a cop, Chloe understood how hard it was to be taken seriously in such a male-dominated field.

"Nineteen-year-old female. Name's Sarah Millfield." Dana took a sip from the mug on her desk. "She called nine-one-one at twenty-two hundred hours to report a break-in. When officers showed up to check it out, they noticed ligature marks on her wrists. They searched the apartment and found pieces of rope tied to the headboard and blood on the sheets. She refused to give a statement to the officers, so they called me in." Dana took another sip and shrugged. "I managed to coax her down here to the station. But she won't consent to a medical exam, and now she's not even talking to me."

"No injuries other than the ligature marks?"

Dana shook her head. "None that I can see."

"You said there was blood on the sheets. How much?"

Somber eyes regarded her as Dana thought about the question and probably what it meant. "Not much."

She nodded. "Okay." The blood on the sheets was probably from the assault. "Where is she?"

"Upstairs. Room eight." Dana stood and headed toward her own desk across the room to grab a ringing telephone. "Go ahead. I'm right behind you."

Chloe made her way through the station and up the stairs, getting several nods and innocent winks from the familiar faces she passed. Wearing a charcoal blazer with matching slacks and a plain, forest green mock-turtle, she was accustomed to hiding her femininity in order to discourage unwanted advances from the men she worked with. As an attractive woman in law enforcement, the last thing she wanted was to be seen as one.

Her own mother had cursed her with blond curly locks, full lips, and a body fit for the cover of *Playboy*. Most men lost about fifty IQ points whenever she walked into a room, but she found that the detectives here were different than most men. It appeared as though they genuinely respected her. She figured it had something to do with Dana and the way she commanded respect from her peers by achieving that balance between strong and beautiful. In a sense, Dana had already paved the way.

The detectives here were a tight-knit group. Most had been working together for a number of years, their passion for solving cases and putting the bad guys behind bars made clear by the long hours they worked without complaint. Strangely enough, Chloe had found it wasn't a tough group to break into at all. She'd prepared herself for a long and tedious battle to win their respect and gain their trust but was shocked when they readily accepted her and her expertise pretty much from the get-go.

Every Friday night, their entire unit would hit the local cop hangout, commiserate about the week's caseload, play some pool, and drink themselves into oblivion. And every Friday without fail, they'd invite Chloe to tag along. For three full months, she'd managed to dodge their invitations. But she was running out of excuses. She knew she'd have to relent at some point and start letting people in again. She just didn't feel ready to do that yet. Her walls were there with good reason.

Standing outside the interview room, Chloe leaned against the glass, crossed her arms, and watched the young woman inside. Sarah was curled in a ball on one of the chairs, picking at a string on the sleeve of her gray Boston College sweatshirt. Her eyes were red-rimmed, puffy, and haunted. There was a small split in her lower lip and a fresh bruise just beginning to form on her right cheekbone. Red hair, pale, freckled. She looked so young and afraid.

Chloe straightened as footsteps sounded on the stairs behind her. Dana joined her at the glass, and they both looked in on the girl.

Long seconds passed. Dana was the one to break the silence. "Rumor has it you have some kind of magic to get victims talking." She pierced Chloe with a steady gaze. "So what's your secret?"

She swore those dark eyes could see straight through to all her private thoughts and fears. Of course, it was ridiculous to think that was even possible, but she found herself avoiding the eye contact just the same. "No magic. I just sit with them."

She stepped to the door and paused with her fingers curled around the door handle just long enough to take a deep breath. No matter how many times she did this, it never got any easier.

Dana watched from behind the glass as Chloe pulled up a chair beside Sarah and sat in silence. Sarah began talking almost instantly. Little by little, the young woman unfolded her body on the chair like a flower, petal by petal, as she opened up to Chloe about what happened.

Dana had tried everything she could think of to get Sarah to talk before she'd resorted to calling Chloe. Absolutely nothing had worked. She'd pulled every single tool from the toolbox she'd assembled over the years as both a cop and a detective. She liked to think she was good at building a rapport with people in general, but victims especially. She now found herself suddenly questioning her skill set.

Regardless, she was glad Chloe was there. BPD had obviously made the right call with hiring her. She shook her head in amazement. Watching Chloe, she decided, was like watching a magician up close and still not gaining insight into how the slight of hand actually worked.

The feeling of having seen Chloe somewhere before was even stronger now. Every time she tried to corner the memory of Chloe's face, it just evaporated. Maybe she should simply ask her. On second thought...*Gee, haven't we seen each other somewhere before?* sounded too much like a come-on line. Scratch that. She'd have to figure this one out on her own.

Chapter Two

Chloe watched the passing traffic from the passenger's seat as Dana sped through the city. At 5:56 a.m., the sky was just beginning to lighten.

She thought about poor Sarah and everything she'd gone through in the last twelve hours. Through intermittent sobs, Sarah had shared her story. She'd even consented to an exam, her only request that Chloe stay and hold her hand until it was over.

Dana pulled in to the department's lot, parked alongside another patrol car, and withdrew the keys from the ignition. She looked over at Chloe. "You okay?" Dana placed a hand on her arm and gave it a gentle squeeze.

She stiffened under the touch. "Fine. Just tired." They'd driven back from the hospital in silence, Sarah's assault heavy in the air between them.

"Why don't you go on home and get some rest? You can tackle the paperwork later with fresh eyes."

Chloe knew herself well enough to realize an unfiled report would keep her from falling asleep. "No"—she shook her head—"I'll come in and finish it now."

Dana sighed, studying her. "After a night like that, we need to decompress. It's too early for alcohol." She made a point of leaning over and looking down at Chloe's shoes.

Chloe followed her gaze to her black leather brogues. Fashionably conservative, she made a point of always wearing comfortable flats. She didn't believe in heels, especially on the job. You just never knew when you might have to chase the bad guys or, alternatively, run from them.

Dana grinned. "Race you to the fourth floor?"

Never one to turn down a challenge, Chloe narrowed her eyes. "What are the stakes?"

"Loser makes coffee."

"I take mine with cream and two sugars," Chloe said without skipping a beat. She knew she was fast.

"French vanilla creamer. No sugar." Dana winked. "Ready?"

She nodded.

"On three. One…"

They both opened their car doors and glanced back at each other.

"Two…three!"

Chloe leaped up, slammed her door shut, and took off with Dana close on her heels. They sprinted across the parking lot toward the brick building that housed the Boston PD. The door swung open when they were still about fifty yards away. A uniformed police officer stepped out, saving her the trouble of scanning her keycard to gain entry. Still sprinting, she held up her badge and identified herself to the officer to avoid startling him.

"Hey, Fred!" Dana called out from behind.

"Hiya, Dana," he said, stepping aside to let them pass. "What's the hurry?"

"Coffee," they both said in unison.

"Must be damn good coffee. Hey, save me a cup!" he shouted after them.

Chloe flew up the stairs two at a time. They were neck and neck now, but she had the advantage of the inside railing. She used it to pull herself up even faster. They reached the second floor landing at the same time, both breathing hard as they continued their ascent.

"First one to touch the door," Dana said beside her.

Chloe was at least a good few feet ahead by the time they approached the third floor landing. She had saved just enough energy for a burst of speed up the final flight of stairs. She was halfway to the fourth floor when Dana caught up with her. Clambering up the stairs as fast as their legs would carry them, they both reached for the door. Chloe watched helplessly as Dana's fingertips grazed the door's metal surface microseconds before hers.

Breathing hard, they stood there, hands on hips, sizing each other up. Clearly, Dana would make a great running partner. Chloe had a sudden and unexpected longing to take her walls down—just a little—to make a new friend. Having shut everyone out from her old life two years ago, she was admittedly out of practice in the fine art of interpersonal communication. She decided now was as good a time as any to make the leap. "Run after work?" she asked between breaths.

Dana just stared at her but didn't answer right away.

Feeling awkward and uncomfortable, she looked from Dana to the floor.

"Depends," Dana finally said, still out of breath.

Chloe looked up. "On what?"

"We do five miles and then a sprint at the end. Loser buys pizza."

Chloe smiled. "You're on." She had no intention of losing to Dana twice in one day. Whatever happened, she decided it was still a win-win. Sharing pizza with a friend was something she suddenly found herself looking forward to.

❖

Coffee in each hand, Chloe was carefully making her way across the room to Dana's desk when she saw him. His Armani suit and tie were flawless, his black shoes shiny enough to reflect the overhead fluorescents and serve as beacons to incoming aircraft. Their eyes locked, and he smiled in recognition. He was being escorted upstairs by a uniformed officer, but there must have been some mistake. The interview rooms were upstairs. Those rooms were only used for victims or witnesses of a crime—never for suspects. Her eyes darted to his hands. No handcuffs.

Which meant he was free to go after they interviewed him.

Bile rose in her throat. *Oh God, no.* What was he doing here? She'd moved clear across the state to eliminate even the possibility of running into him. She felt the blood drain from her face as he rounded the corner and vanished from sight. When she finally managed to tear her eyes from the stairwell, she caught Dana studying her intently just a few feet away. Relief washed over her as her eyes met Dana's. A safe, friendly face.

Hot coffee sloshed from each mug as she set them down on Dana's desk with shaky hands. Chloe struggled mightily to regain her composure. It took every ounce of willpower not to make a mad dash to her car and drive as far away as she could get. "Be right back." She turned and headed to the locker room in an effort to avoid the probing eyes of the detective.

The locker room was deserted. She made a beeline for one of the bathroom stalls and emptied the contents of her stomach in one violent heave.

The door to the locker room swung open on squeaky hinges and banged against the wall. For several terrifying seconds, Chloe was convinced it was him. She held her breath and listened, wishing she had died that day to spare herself the terror of now. The terror of what she was about to face.

"Chloe?" Dana's voice sounded cautious and concerned on the other side of the stall door. "Everything okay?"

Chloe let out her breath and fumbled with the lock. Sweating and shaking, she mumbled something about not feeling well. She stepped over to the sink to rinse her mouth and splash her face with cold water. Lifting her head, she caught her own reflection in the mirror as water ran off the tip of her nose. She barely recognized herself. Wisps of blond hair clung to her forehead. Dark hazel eyes were now the color of smoke and ripe with panic.

Dana said something behind her she couldn't quite make out. The *lub-dub* of her own heart beating triple-time filled her ears and all but consumed her senses. She cast her eyes to the door, afraid that at any minute he would burst in and make her worst nightmare a reality. Again.

She leaned over the sink because she thought she was going to be sick. Her knees suddenly buckled. Arms closed around her as she slid to the tile. Disgusted at the thought of him touching her, she tried desperately to push away and grab for her gun. There was a brief struggle as they fought to see who would gain control. But then she heard Dana's voice, firm and soothing in her ear.

Chloe looked up, confused. It was Dana there with her, not him. When she tried to stand, Dana's face started to blacken around the edges. Her arms grew tingly, and she felt strangely disconnected from her body...lightheaded, fuzzy.

She fought to hold on to consciousness for as long as she could before she realized she just didn't care anymore. Didn't have the strength to fight anymore. For the second time in her life, she embraced the idea of falling into a dark and bottomless slumber—a place where her pain, fears, and grief would finally be subdued.

She felt her body sag against Dana's, aware only of the freedom that came with not caring. She filled her lungs with air. *This is going to be my last breath*, she thought, relieved, and she let it out like a caged bird taking flight.

❖

Sitting beside Chloe's hospital bed, Dana's mind raced. What the hell happened? After quizzing Dana with some questions, the doctor explained that Chloe had experienced a vasovagal response, also known as neurocardiogenic syncope, where the heart rate and blood pressure suddenly drop. He went on to say it was probably a reaction to extreme emotional distress. He'd administered a mild sedative. Chloe would sleep it off and most likely wake up in a few hours, fully recovered.

Which meant Dana had a few hours to try to tease this out. It had all started with that man at the station. She'd watched from her desk as Chloe locked eyes with him across the room. Clearly recognizing her from somewhere, he'd smiled. It was the most chilling smile Dana had ever seen. There was no warmth in it whatsoever.

Chloe had instantly frozen in place as she watched him being led upstairs. In that moment, she'd reminded Dana of an injured gazelle cornered by a ravenous lion. Briefly turning her attention to Dana as he vanished from sight, she looked like she'd just seen a ghost.

When she hurried off to the locker room, Dana had decided to go after her. Something wasn't right. Her instincts told her Chloe was in trouble.

Chloe had exited from the bathroom stall, looking pale and shaky. It was clear she was terrified but trying hard to pretend everything was fine. Dana caught her in midair as she'd started to faint. She shuddered as she recalled Chloe drawing her weapon. Dana had wrestled it from her grasp quickly and quietly, aware of the trouble Chloe would be in if fellow officers were alerted to the scuffle. Then, without warning, she had stopped breathing. When Dana initiated CPR, she couldn't help but notice the scars on her breasts.

Bite marks.

They were in the exact same location as the bite marks on Gabbi. She was sure of it. She'd seen them herself before the medical examiner took possession of Gabbi's body. That had to be more than coincidence.

She sighed. What the hell did it all mean? Was this connected in some way to Gabbi's case? She watched the steady rise and fall of Chloe's chest as she slept. Convinced something more was going on here, she withdrew her cell and dialed Maribel's number.

Maribel answered on the first ring. "Sorry I'm late. Got stuck in a meeting with a witness."

Dana looked at her watch and remembered they were supposed to meet for lunch. "Turns out, I can't make it today."

"Something must be wrong for you to pass up a date with the burrito man."

"I'm at the hospital—"

"Where? Are you okay?"

"I'm fine. I'm with a colleague."

"Who?"

Dana stood and walked over to close the door for some privacy. "Chloe Maddox," she whispered.

"She okay?"

Dana explained what the doctor had told her. She also took her through the events as they unfolded at the station. She knew Maribel would keep everything in confidence. "I need a favor." She didn't want to ask someone from the department to look into this in an official capacity. Her instincts were usually right on the mark, but she couldn't risk bringing Chloe's reputation into question or damaging her career in any way.

"You want me to find out why she left Martha's Vineyard," Maribel guessed.

Dana smiled, grateful to have a friend she knew she could trust with anything. "I might start with a call to her last commanding officer."

"I'm on it. I'll get back to you as soon as I know something."

❖

The first thing Chloe became aware of was the smell of disinfectant. She opened her eyes to a dimly lit hospital room and found herself in bed with a blood pressure cuff, IV, oxygen, and electrodes on her chest. She followed the wires out from the sleeve of her hospital gown and up to the monitor beside the bed. She watched the jagged green lines on the screen in silence. Heart rate fifty. Blood pressure one ten over seventy—

"You're awake." Dana rubbed her eyes and leaned forward from the chair on the other side of the bed.

Chloe pulled the oxygen cannula away from her nose and set it aside. "How long have I been here?"

Dana looked at her watch. "About six hours. We're at Mass General. The doctor said you had a vasovagal response. It's when the vagus nerve is—

"I know what it is." She was well aware the vagus nerve was the longest cranial nerve in the body, reaching from the brain through the neck and all the way down into the abdomen. With parasympathetic fibers, it could slow the heart rate dramatically when stimulated and cause a major system shutdown. Most law enforcement officers were trained to trigger the vagus nerve when dealing with a dangerous suspect by delivering a quick, hard jab to the side of the neck. It was used only as a last resort because such a blow could result in a sudden drop in blood pressure and be fatal. Times of severe stress had also been known to cause a similar reaction. And today probably fell into that severe stress category, Chloe thought angrily, remembering the Armani suit and shiny shoes worn to conceal the monster underneath.

"Has anything like that ever happened to you before?" Dana asked.

Chloe shook her head and sat up slowly.

"How are you feeling?"

"Better now. Thanks."

"Want me to see if I can find the doctor?"

"No." As much as she appreciated that Dana had waited with her, she wanted her to go now. She offered a reassuring smile. "I'll be fine. I'm sure you have more important things to do than sit around here babysitting me. Go on home."

But Dana didn't budge. "You almost died, Chloe."

She felt Dana's eyes searching her face for a hint of emotion. Strangely, she felt nothing. Only the vaguest regret that she was here having this conversation at all.

"How much do you remember?"

Chloe shrugged, feigning ignorance. "I remember feeling pretty sick."

"Okay. Here's what I remember." Dana sat on the edge of the bed. "There was a man brought in for questioning in connection with a case I'm working. I saw you watching him." She paused. "You turned white as a ghost and ran to the bathroom."

She refused to give Dana the reaction she was obviously expecting and forced her face to remain expressionless.

"I saw him look at you and smile," Dana went on, "like he knew you."

Chloe swallowed. "I honestly have no idea who you're talking about. When I started feeling sick, it came on pretty quick. I was probably looking in his direction when it hit me."

Dana studied her, freely roaming her face for a chink in the armor, her dark brown eyes full of skepticism and concern. "You stopped breathing in the bathroom, and your heart rate took a nosedive. I removed your shirt to do CPR. I saw the bite marks on your breasts...here and here." She pointed to two places on the outside of Chloe's hospital gown. "Did he do that to you?"

She said nothing and hugged the blanket closer to her body, feeling more uncomfortable by the minute.

Dana's cell phone rang. She stood from the bed, reached down, and unclipped it from her belt.

❖

"Are you still there with her?" Maribel asked.

"Still here," Dana said.

"Is she awake? Can she hear you?"

"Yep."

"Have you asked her about what happened yet?"

"I have." Dana was trying to be as vague as possible. She didn't want Chloe to know this call was about her.

"And?"

"And then you called."

"Oh. Sorry about that." Maribel paused on the other end. "Let me just start by saying you're definitely in the right line of work. Your instincts are beyond extraordinary."

"Good to know. What did you find out?"

"Her old captain gave me an earful. He said Chloe was one of the best cops he ever had. Works harder than everyone else, follows the rules, and she has great instincts. Reminds me of someone else I know."

"That all he gave you?"

Maribel sighed. "Chloe was abducted two years ago. She was dumped in front of her old department twenty-five days later, beaten to a bloody pulp and barely alive. She was in a coma for a week. When she woke up, she couldn't remember anything about the abduction. All of her other memories were intact, but she couldn't remember a single detail about what happened. Her captain said they had a hunch about who did it but no evidence. So the case went cold pretty fast."

Dana had learned over the years to pay attention to the instincts of fellow cops. A simple hunch could be the stepping stone to solving a case. "Did he give you a name?"

"He did. It's the same man you saw staring at Chloe this morning: Sylvio Caprazzio."

She was impressed. Looked like the Tisbury PD had cops with good instincts.

"I'm on my way to you now," Maribel went on. "I think I have a way to get Chloe to start talking about this."

"How?" Dana asked, suddenly curious.

"I'll show you when I get there. See you in a few."

Chapter Three

Chloe shifted uncomfortably. She had a feeling the phone call was about her.

Dana's eyes found hers again as she ended the call and sat back down on the edge of the bed. "Is there anything you'd like to share with me?"

"No." Her back bristled. She didn't like where this was headed. Dana was treating her like a victim.

"That man at the station…" Dana blinked once, twice, never taking her eyes from Chloe's. "Did you recognize him as the man who abducted you?"

Chloe took a breath to steady herself. "I'd like you to leave." She pressed the call button for the nurse. She needed to get out of here. Now.

Dana remained on the edge of the bed and made no move to honor her wishes. "You've interviewed dozens of victims since you joined the BPD. Everyone talks about how you have this way of getting inside a victim's head. You seem to know just the right thing to say to get their walls to come down." She sighed. "What would you say if you were in my shoes right now?"

A young nurse rapped softly on the door and poked her head inside. "You're awake. How are you feeling?"

"Better." Chloe held up her arm with the IV. "Can you take this out?"

"I'll have to clear it with the doctor first—"

"Take it out now, or I'll take it out myself."

The young nurse frowned as she looked back and forth between her and Dana, obviously sensing the tension. "Give me a minute, and I'll take care of it." She withdrew her head from the doorway and disappeared.

"Talk to me, Chloe."

"There's nothing to talk about." She reached over with her free hand and peeled the sticky tape from the IV. In one fluid motion, she ripped out the catheter and held her arm until the bleeding stopped. She felt underneath her gown for the electrodes and peeled them off. "Where are my clothes?" she asked without looking up.

Dana stood, walked to the closet, and withdrew a plastic bag. She tossed the bag on the bed and turned so her back was to Chloe. "Go ahead and change. I'm not leaving."

Well, I sure as hell am. Furious, Chloe climbed out of bed, stepped into her pants, and fastened her bra. She'd just slipped out of her hospital gown and into her shirt when there was another knock at the door.

Without waiting for a reply, Maribel Murphy opened the hospital room door and stepped inside. She set her briefcase in a chair and walked up to Chloe. Her dark eyes, fair skin, auburn hair, and high cheekbones—combined with her telltale last name—left little doubt about her Irish heritage. She was dressed to kill in a power suit and black high heels. "Are you all right?"

"I'm fine. Just overtired," Chloe lied.

"Dana says you're refusing to talk about what happened two years ago."

"That's because there's nothing to talk about."

"I've been doing this a long time, Chloe." She glanced at Dana. "We both have. Give us a little more credit than flat-out denial."

Chloe put her hands on her hips and held her ground. She had no intention of opening this can of worms anywhere but in the privacy of her own mind.

Maribel withdrew a folder from her briefcase, opened it, and dumped about thirty photos on the bed.

Mortified, Chloe leaned over to pick one up. "How'd you get these?"

"Contacted the Tisbury PD. They still have it on file as an unsolved case. Your former captain told me you were abducted in the middle of the night after your fiancé was murdered. He said your abductor kept you for twenty-five days. You turned up later, half-dead."

Chloe felt the heat rising in her cheeks. "What else did he say?"

"That you were beaten so badly you suffered total memory loss of what happened. Your inability to recover those memories impeded their investigation, forcing them to put it on ice until further notice."

Chloe couldn't help but stare at the photos. Bruised, swollen, bloodied and broken, there wasn't a single inch of her body spared.

Dana stepped over and picked up several photos that had fallen to the tile. One by one, she collected them—gently, almost reverently. Dana stood, studying the photos in her hands with an intensity that surprised Chloe. "My God, Chloe." She finally looked up, a tangled expression of rage and disbelief on her face. "Did that bastard at the station do this to you?"

She hesitated, but only briefly. "Yes."

Maribel stepped closer. "Your former captain said they had a person of interest, but you were never able to make a positive ID. What changed?"

Chloe shook her head and sighed, resigned to the fact that these two women were obviously too intelligent and intuitive to be shaken off her trail so easily. She might as well come clean.

"The memories started returning a few months ago…just after I was hired at the BPD."

"Why didn't you contact one of the detectives at your old house?" Dana asked.

"Because the memories are scattered. They come in bits and pieces. I was waiting until…" She trailed off, unable to put her thoughts into words. A perfectionist by nature, she wanted to be able to recall everything that happened during those twenty-five days as accurately as humanly possible. She longed to provide the details that would warrant reopening the case—the details that felt tantalizingly close but were still somehow just beyond her reach.

"You were waiting until all the pieces fit together," Dana finished for her. "You wanted to have everything straight in your own head before reopening the case. I get it. I'd do exactly the same."

Chloe looked up from the floor and met Dana's gaze, grateful for their connection.

"How much do you remember?" Maribel asked.

"There are a lot of blank spaces I'm still trying to fill in," she admitted. "When I saw him at the station this morning, more came back." She squeezed her eyes shut against the images inside her own mind. "But not everything. It's been pretty much a steady trickle day by day."

"Has anyone been helping you remember?" Dana asked. "A therapist…someone like that?"

She shook her head. "I wanted to remember things on my own. I didn't want a defense attorney claiming my memories were manufactured by an outside influence."

Dana stepped closer. "So you've been facing this all alone?"

"I haven't been alone," she said, touched by Dana's concern. "I have Taz."

"Who's Taz?" Maribel and Dana asked in unison.

"My German shepherd. He's a trained attack dog. He goes everywhere with me." She could feel the pity oozing from each of the women standing before her as tangibly as if it was solid matter. "I've been dealing just fine," she assured them. "I'm strong. I can handle this on my own."

"Well, now you don't have to." Maribel wrapped her hand around Chloe's arm and gave it a squeeze. "Dana and I are in this with you from here on out."

"Every step," Dana added. "We can help you remember more."

"Do you have enough right now to make an ID?" Maribel pressed.

Chloe nodded as she looked Maribel square in the eye. "I *know* it's him. There's no doubt in my mind."

"Okay. My office will bring charges against him forthwith. In the meantime"—Maribel turned to Dana—"she shouldn't be alone."

"I'll be fine," Chloe argued. "I promise not to fall apart."

"I'm not worried about that. I'm worried about him and the threat he poses to you once he's charged. I'll fight like hell to make sure he stays behind bars pending trial. But this guy has plenty of money, and I'm sure he'll hire the best defense money can buy. Bail could very well be granted."

Chloe said nothing because she realized Maribel was right. She knew firsthand how dangerous Sylvio was. If he knew his freedom was in jeopardy, she had no doubt he'd come after her.

"I'll stay with her," Dana offered. "I can use my vacation time."

"You don't have to—"

"I want to," Dana said, cutting her off. She met Chloe's eyes with razor-sharp determination. "Like Maribel said, we're in this together."

"Besides, Dana hasn't used a vacation day in..." Maribel looked to Dana. "How long has it been?"

"Five years next month. Captain threatened to buy me a ticket to the Bahamas and have me escorted to the airport in handcuffs. He'll be happy about this, believe me. It won't be a vacation, of course, but it'll look that way on the books. That's all he cares about."

Chloe looked down at the floor as she fought back tears. These two women were pretty extraordinary. She realized how fortunate she was in that moment to have them by her side.

Dana cleared her throat. "There's one condition."

Chloe looked up. "What's that?"

"Taz can't eat me."

She smiled through the tears. "I can't make any promises, but if you have some goat cheese handy, you'll make a friend for life."

"Goat cheese?" Dana asked, frowning. "What self-respecting attack dog eats goat cheese?"

Dana texted dispatch, and soon a familiar face from their station emerged from an unmarked car outside the hospital. Hunter threw the keys to Dana and sauntered up to Chloe.

"How're you feeling, Chloe? Everyone's worried about you."

"Better now. Too much coffee, not enough water," she lied.

Hunter patted his gut and laughed. "Too many doughnuts, not enough veggies."

Chloe couldn't help but smile. She'd liked the guy from the moment they'd met. He reminded her of Jim Belushi in the movie *K-9*.

A patrol car pulled up alongside Hunter. He climbed in, slammed the door, and rolled down his window. "Where are you ladies off to now?"

"Working a case," was all Dana offered.

Hunter thrust his chin out as the car pulled forward. "Be safe out there."

Dana opened the passenger's door on the silver Ford Focus and motioned for her to get inside. Chloe stared up at the sky from her window as Dana walked around to the driver's side and slipped behind the wheel.

Thick, dark clouds roiled overhead, waving their fists and threatening the day with afternoon showers. Chloe nestled her hands between her thighs for warmth. Already halfway through November, Thanksgiving was just over a week away. "Where are we going?" she asked, lowering her gaze to the stop sign ahead.

Dana rolled through the stop sign and swung into the far left lane on the one-way street. "We'll make a quick stop at your place so you can pack some clothes, grab Taz, and then head over to my house. You two can spend the night in my guest room."

Chloe glanced down and noticed for the first time that her badge was missing from the front of her blazer. No gun. No badge. She felt naked. "Did my badge and gun go on strike for higher wages and better working conditions?"

Dana laughed. "I have them."

"I'd like them back."

The air between them grew suddenly heavy. "Not yet."

Chloe felt her anger rising to the surface. "Why the hell not?"

Dana pulled to the side of the road, cut the engine, and turned to her. "You went for your gun in the bathroom and tried to draw on me. I can't return your weapon until I'm confident something like that isn't going to happen again."

Chloe met her gaze, haunted by the sudden memory of doing just what Dana said she did. "Oh my God, I'm sorry. I didn't mean—"

"I know you didn't, which is why I didn't tell anyone about it. That's between us." She smiled reassuringly. "Just don't shoot me anytime soon, and no one will be the wiser."

They parked in the driveway of Chloe's condo twenty minutes later. Dana told her to sit tight while she went in to have a look around.

"Do you have a death wish?"

Already out of the car, Dana opened the rear door and bent over to look back in at her. "What?"

"Taz is waiting inside," Chloe reminded her.

Dana reached into the back seat, withdrew a small plastic container, and held it up. "Goat cheese."

"Where'd you get that?"

"Hospital cafeteria." Dana grinned, obviously proud of herself.

"Doesn't matter. He'll still tear you to pieces."

Dana frowned. "But I have goat cheese."

Chloe shook her head. Dana clearly didn't know anything about German shepherds. "I have to introduce you first. Otherwise, he'll think you're an intruder, and you'll have to shoot him. You and I will no longer be friends if you kill my dog." Chloe waited patiently as Dana pondered the situation. "Besides, I have a state-of-the-art security system in addition to the attack dog. I highly doubt anyone is waiting inside to ambush me."

"Fine. You win. We go in together."

Chloe opened her car door and climbed out. She walked past Dana and up the brick steps to the door of her condo. Taz barked viciously on the other side of the door, alerting her to the fact that something wasn't right. The hair on the back of her neck stood up as she pressed her index finger against a side panel to disengage the alarm system. She was hurriedly turning the key in the lock when a bullet blasted a hole in the door. With lightning-quick reflexes, Dana shoved her inside and pushed her to the floor.

Dana was on top of her, now nose to nose with Taz. He bared his teeth menacingly and growled deep in his throat. "Goat cheese," Dana whispered frantically. "I have goat cheese."

Chloe gave Taz the command to stand down and back away as she and Dana dove around the corner.

Dana drew her gun, snapped the safety off. "You hurt?"

"No." She was just about to ask the same when her eyes caught the torn, bloody sleeve of Dana's sweater. "Now might be a good time to give me back my gun."

Dana remained silent and studied her for long seconds as they both listened for signs of the shooter. Chloe's mind was spinning. Had Sylvio returned to kill her? Was their encounter in the station a warning that he was coming for her? She frowned. Sylvio seemed too careful and meticulous to go around shooting at her in broad daylight. He was the type of psychopath who planned every detail well in advance and savored the long drawn-out suffering of his victims. She didn't know for a fact there were other victims. She was just making an educated guess. Men like Sylvio lived for the thrill of watching others suffer.

Waiting obediently a few feet away, Taz's entire body was on high alert. He was focused on something outside. She could tell from the tension in his body he was ready to spring into action. Chloe instructed him to lie down. He did.

Dana finally reached under her sweater and pulled out a gun from the small of her back. She handed it over, tossed the badge to go with it, and unclipped her cell from her belt to call in for backup.

Chloe clipped the badge to the outside of her blazer. Taz flattened his ears, bared his teeth, and growled in warning, his attention still on something—or someone—just outside the door. Chloe caught movement out of the corner of her eye. She had to find a way to get this door closed and put a solid barricade between them and the shooter—preferably without exposing her body and making herself an easy target.

There was an umbrella stand within reach. She grabbed an umbrella and used the curved handle to hook the door as a 9 mm came into view just beyond the door's threshold. It was fitted with a silencer. Two more bullets sailed through the air. One embedded itself in the wall. The other pierced the umbrella and lodged itself in the wood floor. She finally managed to shut the door the rest of the way. The lock automatically engaged.

Dana ended the call. "You hit?"

"No." Chloe tossed the umbrella aside and shook out her stinging hands. The bullet had ricocheted off the metal rod inside the umbrella. The impact had radiated out to both hands. Taz whined and army crawled over to her.

"Backup's on the way."

Chloe nodded, reassured Taz with a scratch under his chin, and lifted her gun from the floor. She noticed some red spatters on the wall and a few drops on the carpet. Dana's blood.

They stared at one another in silence and listened intently as rain smacked the pavement outside. Chloe draped an arm around Taz to keep him close. They couldn't cross the living room. Too many windows. Their best bet, Chloe knew, was to stay put and wait until backup arrived.

CHAPTER FOUR

With lights and sirens blazing, several BPD squad cars gunned their engines down Chloe's street and came to a screeching halt in front of the condo. Sirens from additional units erupted in the distance. Whenever one of their own was the target of a shooter, Chloe knew it was all hands on deck.

On Dana's orders, uniformed police officers scoured the immediate property, then spread to the surrounding neighborhoods, posting checkpoints and lookouts within a two mile radius. Neither Chloe nor Dana had heard a vehicle engine before or after the shooting. Whether the shooter was on foot, or had merely parked out of earshot of Chloe's condo, he could be anywhere. But if anyone could flush him out, it was the Boston Police.

All they had to go on was Chloe's eyewitness account of the shooter's weapon, his black leather jacket, and her mental image of his hand. It wasn't much, but at least it was something.

After giving their statements, Dana, Chloe, and Taz remained safely inside the condo.

"You're sure it wasn't Sylvio's hand?" Dana asked, sitting on the sofa opposite Chloe.

"Positive. The shooter's hand was smaller. And his knuckles were hairier," she added, after giving it more thought. Sylvio's hands would forever be ingrained in her mind—the single memory she had never lost in the two years since her abduction. "Shooter's timing is awfully coincidental."

"I don't believe in coincidence," Dana replied, echoing her thoughts exactly. "Sylvio's behind this."

Taz returned from his water bowl in the kitchen and stationed himself beside Chloe, his eyes intent on Dana. When Dana returned the eye contact, he lowered his head and growled.

"Now might be a good time to get the goat cheese," Chloe suggested.

"I left it over there." Dana threw a glance at the kitchen table but made no motion to move. "Am I allowed to get up?"

Chloe laughed. "Of course."

"I don't know why you're laughing." Dana mistakenly made eye contact with Taz once again. Less forgiving the second time, he bared his teeth in warning. "It's like staring down the barrel of a loaded gun...with the safety off," Dana said, careful to look only at Chloe. "Where'd you get this dog, anyway?"

"I told you," she said evasively. "He's a guard dog."

"From where?"

Chloe hesitated. "K-9 training."

"How'd you manage to get your hands on a police dog? They spend thousands on training those dogs. Departments keep them on the job until they're at least, what, seven or eight? I'm no dog expert, but Taz doesn't look old enough to be retired."

Chloe realized then what a great detective Dana must be in the field. Seemed she could smell something askew a mile away. "They have very rigorous graduation standards." She shrugged. "He didn't quite meet them."

"He flunked out of K-9 school?" Dana asked, looking suddenly worried. "Why'd they flunk him?" she persisted.

"There were just some...minor concerns," Chloe said, waving a hand in the air dismissively and trying not to take offense to the word *flunked*.

"Concerns about what?" Dana laughed. "His mental stability?"

Chloe raised an eyebrow but said nothing, neither confirming nor denying. But that was, in fact, the case.

Dana stopped laughing. "Oh my God. I'm right, aren't I? You adopted a police dog that couldn't make the cut because he's mentally unstable?"

"They were going to euthanize him," Chloe explained. "Nobody wanted him, not even his handler."

"That should have been your first clue," Dana said, crossing her arms. "Handlers always keep their dogs."

"He never bonded with his handler."

"I can see why. He's crazy."

Apparently ramping up his distaste of Dana to full-blown anger, Taz flattened his ears and growled much louder.

"We are *not* taking your crazy dog to my house tonight."

Chloe sighed and turned to Taz. "You're not making a good impression right now, boy." She grabbed him by the sides of his face until he looked into her eyes. "You need to be nice to Dana. She's my friend. Show her you can have better manners. Otherwise, she won't let you come with us, and I'll have to leave you here all alone tonight. Is that what you want?" He whined and licked her on the chin. "Okay." She released him and gave him a little push in Dana's direction. "Go make nice."

Taz took a few steps toward Dana, sat in front of her, and extended his paw in truce.

"You're kidding me." Dana stared at the dog. "He didn't seriously understand everything you just said. That's impossible."

"He's the smartest dog I've ever had. I don't know how much language he understands, but he understands me, my body language. Taz and I have a connection. We just…get each other."

"I'm afraid to move," Dana admitted. "What should I do?"

"Shake his paw."

"What if he tears my face off?"

"He won't."

"How do you know that?"

"Trust me."

"I like having a face, Chloe. It will be really inconvenient if I don't have one anymore."

"Shake his damn paw before he starts thinking you're a coward."

Dana scooted forward ever so slightly on the sofa. When Taz didn't react, she reached out tentatively to make contact. He obliged by lifting his paw higher, allowing Dana to give it a good, firm shake.

"Good boy," Chloe called out encouragingly as Dana released his paw. "Show her you can be trusted." Taz glanced back at her over his shoulder. "Go ahead," she insisted.

He inched forward slowly and laid his head in Dana's lap. Chloe watched his eyebrows twitch as he patiently waited for Dana to stroke him.

"Should I pet him?" Dana asked, visibly tense.

"Yes. You can relax now. He's accepted you."

Dana reached out to stroke the top of his head. "Okay, maybe you can stay at my house tonight. Would you like that?"

Taz lifted his head from Dana's lap to give her hand a little lick.

"So that's it?" Dana asked, looking to Chloe. "Taz and I are friends now?"

"Some goat cheese would definitely seal the deal."

Taz's tail began wagging furiously at the mention of goat cheese. He stood and led Dana to the kitchen high-top table. His nose had obviously pinpointed the container's location.

Dana peeled back the lid and dutifully fed the goat cheese to Taz, piece by piece. She pressed the lid back snugly in place.

Taz shook his head and snorted in protest. Dana just stared at him. When she didn't pick up on the cue, he remained seated, looked her square in the eye, and chuffed.

She turned to Chloe. "What's he saying?"

"He knows there's more cheese in there."

"Oh." Dana returned her gaze to Taz. "I'm saving it for later. That okay with you?"

Taz let out a high-pitched bark.

"Fine," Dana said, peeling back the lid once again. "But don't come complaining to me later if you get a tummy ache."

Confident the two were getting along just fine now, Chloe left them alone for a few minutes to pack an overnight bag. By the time she returned, Dana was sitting on the floor. Taz was sprawled out in front of her, and she was giving him a belly rub. With his long tongue hanging from the side of his mouth, it looked like he was enjoying every minute of it.

They agreed they were too tired to cook and decided to stop for pizza on the way to Dana's. "I know a great Greek-style pizza joint not far from here," Dana said.

"Perfect." Her mouth was already watering in anticipation. She was starving. "Greek is my favorite."

"Mine too. Toppings?"

"I prefer plain cheese, but I can be flexible."

"I like plain, too." Dana held her gaze momentarily from the driver's seat.

Chloe checked the clock on the dash: 6:05 p.m. Night was fully upon them now. Daylight savings had stopped a few weeks ago, so the days were now shorter and colder. She studied Dana in the light of oncoming traffic and realized how truly beautiful she was.

They arrived at Dana's ten minutes later. Two patrol cars sat out front, one in the driveway. Uniformed officers would take turns circling Dana's house on foot throughout the night. Chloe didn't envy them. It was supposed to dip into the twenties later.

She and Taz followed Dana to the front door of an enormous colonial revival house. Dana flipped a light switch as they stepped inside the large foyer.

Chloe gasped. "This is gorgeous!" Wide-plank hardwood floors, white wainscoting, and elegantly patterned yellow wallpaper greeted her. An immense staircase with a curved mahogany banister led to the second floor, and a rounded white archway with recessed panels led to a spacious living room straight ahead. The room was accented with white crown molding, elegant pilasters, and case trim around all the doors and windows. The house was exquisite, but it wasn't a house. It was a mansion. This place was immense.

"Thanks. My grandfather left me this house about ten years ago. It's been a decade-long project of mine. I just finished renovations over the summer."

Dana led them through a massive living room with vaulted ceilings. She set the pizza box down on an L-shaped white bench table that was built into one corner of an expansive kitchen. Colorfully patterned throw pillows filled the long bench seats on both sides. Chloe stood in place and looked around, taking in all the details. Custom-crafted dark blue cabinets, white backsplash, and pure white granite countertops combined to give the kitchen a unique and wholesome feel.

"Did you bring food for Taz?" Dana asked, readying their plates.

Chloe shook her head. "He refuses to eat dog food, so he eats what I eat."

"Seriously?" Dana turned to look at her in disbelief. "Have you ever owned a dog before?"

"For your information, I've had dogs pretty much my whole life. All of those dogs ate dog food. But Taz, well, he's different," she confided, studying the furry face she'd come to love. Ears at full attention, he stared back at her as if hanging on her every word.

"I don't think of myself as a dog *owner* when it comes to Taz," she went on. "He's too smart for that. He's just…my friend. I know he has my back, and he knows I have his. It's the least complicated relationship I've ever had." She laughed. "Get to know him a little more. You'll see what I mean."

"Should I set a place for him at the table?" Dana mocked, playfully bumping shoulders.

Chloe cut up two slices of pizza into bite-sized morsels, grabbed a plate off the counter, and set it on the kitchen floor. As usual, Taz sat in front of the plate but didn't touch the food.

"He doesn't want it?" Dana asked.

"He loves pizza. He's just waiting until I start eating."

Dana kept glancing at Taz and his untouched plate of pizza. "Did you teach him to do that?"

"He did it on his own a few days after I adopted him. I think it's an alpha thing. He's showing me respect because I'm the alpha. In a pack, the alpha always eats first."

Dana shook her head and returned her attention to setting the table. "Taz, you are definitely an unusual dog."

His tail wagged at the mention of his name. He followed Chloe with his eyes until she sat at the table with Dana. As soon as she took her first bite, he settled down on the floor and began eating his dinner.

❖

With Taz napping on the floor beside her, Chloe made herself comfortable on the living room sofa. She picked up a framed photo from the end table. A gorgeous dark-haired woman with kind brown eyes smiled back at the camera. "Is this your sister?" she asked as Dana made her way from the kitchen to the living room.

"That's my partner."

"How come I've never met her? I thought I knew all the women at the station." The words were already out of Chloe's mouth by the time her brain finished processing what *partner* meant.

Dana handed her a glass of Chardonnay, took a seat on the sofa, and watched her.

"Wait a minute." She felt her face flush with embarrassment. "Not your BPD partner."

"No." Dana smiled, seemingly amused.

Chloe struggled to find something intelligent to say.

"Does that make you uncomfortable?" Dana asked.

"No. I just didn't know you were…" How much deeper could she dig her own hole here?

"A lesbian?" Dana finished for her.

Taken by surprise, Chloe stared at the floor. Dana was gay? She suddenly found herself wondering if the chemistry between them went beyond friendship. She'd felt drawn to Dana with an indescribable intensity from the moment they'd met at the café. Her heart picked up speed as she acknowledged she was attracted to Dana.

"Listen, if this changes things between us and you'd rather be assigned to another detective, I can arrange for that to happen first thing tomorrow. No hard feelings, Chloe." Dana stood from the sofa. "Help yourself to whatever's in the fridge. Guest room's down the hall on the left." She bent down to give Taz a quick pat on the head. "Try and get a good night's sleep. I'll see you both in the morning."

Alone in her bedroom upstairs, Dana shook her head in disbelief. To say Chloe was shocked to discover she was gay was an understatement. For a fleeting moment, she wondered if Chloe was homophobic but quickly dismissed the idea. BPD would have picked up on that in the psych screening as part of their exhaustive application process and background check. They wouldn't have hired her if anything was flagged that even remotely resembled homophobia. She was proud that the department had no tolerance for bigotry of any kind.

Whatever the case, maybe their friendship was over before it had even started. She suddenly found herself feeling more than a little disappointed. Back at the café and the station, she'd felt a real connection with Chloe. Looked like she was wrong.

She dressed for bed and started thinking of Taz as she brushed her teeth. He was quite a character. They had gotten off on the wrong foot, but she was actually starting to like him.

Well, if Chloe was going to let this prevent them from moving forward as friends, it would be a loss to both of them. For Dana, the prospect of having a new friend in her life who was both a runner and a cop was an obvious no-brainer. On a deeper level, she sensed a vulnerability in Chloe that made her want to stay and help in any way she could. Chloe was gearing up to face something incredibly difficult and could use someone in her corner right now. She needed someone she could count on. Dana was willing to be that person.

CHAPTER FIVE

Chloe had drained her wineglass—three times—before she finally got the courage to venture upstairs and knock on Dana's bedroom door. Taz followed closely at her heels.

"Come in."

Her hands shook as she turned the doorknob.

Dressed in a long-sleeved black silk nightshirt that ended just above her knees, Dana stepped out from the master bathroom, toothbrush in hand. She had let her hair down from the ponytail it was in earlier. It fanned out over her shoulders, making her eyes appear even darker than before.

Chloe scanned the bedroom. No sign of the woman in the photo. Maybe Dana had asked her to stay elsewhere for the night. Or maybe they didn't even live together, she thought. She cleared her throat, forced herself to focus. "Do you have a minute?"

"Sure." Dana set her toothbrush down and leaned against the doorframe. "What's up?"

"I'm totally comfortable with you being..."

"A lesbian?" Dana smirked. "It's okay. You can say it. You won't catch it if you say it out loud."

"I already caught it." Oh God, she sounded like a moron. "What I meant to say was..." She'd rehearsed this in her mind, but the wine was catching up. "I've been with a woman before."

"Good for you." There was that amused smile again.

Chloe rubbed her temples. She really was an idiot. "I had this whole thing worked out in my head, but I think I drank too much."

"Well, I appreciate the gesture."

She couldn't help but feel self-conscious as Dana watched her from across the room. Out of the corner of her eye, she saw something drip from Dana's arm to the carpet. She squinted, looked more closely. "You're bleeding."

"Dammit." Dana pressed a hand to her bicep and ducked around the corner, shutting the door behind her.

"I volunteer as a medic with the fire department," she called out. "Want me to take a look?"

"I thought you said you were drunk."

"Well, I wouldn't do a tracheotomy right now." She laughed. "But bandaging I can handle."

Dana opened the door and stood with one hand pressed against the wound on her arm. She'd traded in the black silk nightshirt for a fluffy cream-colored towel, which she now hugged against her body.

Chloe stepped forward and lifted Dana's hand. Blood welled up from the wound where a tacky clot had opened. "This needs stitches."

"I'm too tired to drive to the hospital. Can't you just bandage it up?"

"Fine. Wait here." With Taz by her side, she headed downstairs to find her duffel bag, dug out what she needed, and returned to Dana. "Take a seat. I need to clean it out first." She set the Betadine, gauze, and butterfly strips on the vanity as Dana sat on the edge of the tub.

"You just happened to have those with you?"

Chloe shrugged. "I've gotten into the habit of taking some basic supplies with me wherever I go. You never know when you might need them. Case in point." She slipped on a pair of latex gloves and set to work. "What's your partner's name?" she asked, trying to break the ice.

"Gabriela."

Beautiful name, she thought. "Does she live here with you?"

Dana inhaled sharply as the Betadine worked its magic. "Gabbi was attacked four years ago in the hospital parking lot where she worked. She never made it home alive."

"I'm so sorry." Her heart went out to Dana. "Did they find who did it?"

"Not yet," Dana said sadly.

Chloe held the gauze against the wound, applying pressure to stanch the bleeding. She didn't know how to feel about this news. It was sad and no doubt tragic for Dana. But finding out Gabriela was no longer in the picture opened Chloe's mind to other possibilities. Maybe the connection she felt with Dana really was the beginning of something deeper than friendship.

"Gabbi was an ER nurse. You would've liked her. She talked about medics all the time. She really admired what you guys do out there."

Chloe pulled the gauze away and reached for the first butterfly strip.

"I was there with her in the ICU for three days after the attack, hoping by some miracle she'd pull through," Dana went on. "I felt so lost because there was nothing I could do to help her."

She pressed the last butterfly strip in place, peeled her gloves into a ball, and tossed them in the trash. Crossing her arms, she leaned against the vanity in supportive silence.

"Anyway..." Dana studied her handiwork and looked up. "That was four years ago. I've done a lot of healing since then." She centered dark eyes on Chloe. "You were engaged once. What was his name?"

Chloe felt the lump in her throat immediately. She wondered how Dana had found out about her fiancé when Maribel's words echoed in her ear...*Your former captain told me you were abducted after your fiancé was murdered.* "Michael." She looked away. "His name was Michael."

"What happened?"

She turned away to gather up the extra gauze and butterfly strips. "Make sure you cover that arm before you take a shower. Those strips need to stay dry and in place for at least a week to minimize the chance of scarring."

Dana wrapped her hand gently around Chloe's as she was picking up the last of the gauze. "What happened?" she asked again.

"I can't do this with you right now, Dana."

"Yes, you can. Every time you try to talk about what happened, it'll get a little easier. I promise." Hugging the towel against her body, Dana stood and reached out to tuck a stray lock behind Chloe's ear.

She sighed. "All I have are fleeting images of that night."

"So let's start there."

"Here? Now?" Chloe asked as a last-ditch effort to halt the conversation. "I'm half drunk, and you're half...naked."

"There's an easy fix to at least half of that problem." Dana ducked around the corner and returned seconds later wearing navy blue silk pajamas. "I can't fix the half drunk part, but I will say this from experience: it's much easier to talk about something difficult when you're feeling the effects of alcohol."

It was a hard truth to accept, but instincts told her this was the time to start talking. She looked over at Taz. He was watching her intently from just outside the bathroom. As soon as she made eye contact, he stepped over and nudged her hand gently with his muzzle. He always seemed to know when she needed a little comfort.

❖

Dana made hot cocoa, and they returned to the living room sofa. Taz settled down at Chloe's feet. He looked up and chuffed as she brought the mug to her lips. "I'd offer you some," she told him, "but dogs can't have chocolate. It'll make you sick."

Seemingly satisfied with the explanation, he set his head down over the tops of Chloe's feet and dozed off.

"Do you always do that?"

"Do what?" Chloe asked, looking up from her mug.

"Talk to him like he understands everything you're saying."

"I guess I do." She shrugged. "You think it's silly."

"Not at all. I think it's sweet." Dana took a sip from her mug and laughed. "I'm actually starting to wonder if he really does understand everything you say. I can see why you like him."

Chloe was glad Dana was starting to come around and see Taz in a more favorable light. "How should we start?" she asked, anxious to get this over with.

"Actually, I'm curious…" Dana paused for a moment, seemingly to collect her thoughts. "Did you know Sylvio—had you ever met him—before he abducted you?"

Chloe was surprised by the question. Either Dana was incredibly astute, or she had already read the case file.

Before she could answer, Dana explained, "The reason I'm asking is because it feels like he has a personal vendetta against you. Back at the station, I saw the way he looked at you and smiled. I've been going over that moment again and again in my mind. It wasn't a smile of recognition. It was a smile of intimidation. Like he was plotting his revenge against you for some perceived slight."

Chloe nodded, impressed by Dana's powers of observation. She had pulled Sylvio over for speeding one night. He'd tried to charm his way out of the ticket, but he was doing ninety in a forty-five zone. Giving him that ticket had turned out to be the worst mistake of her life. Three weeks later, he broke into her fiancé's house and changed their lives forever.

"Sylvio's obviously holding on to that. He feels you wronged him, and all of this is just payback." Dana set her mug down and leaned forward on the sofa. "Walk me through what you remember the night he broke into Michael's home."

"It was a Saturday. Michael and I had gone out for dinner at our favorite Italian restaurant. We were celebrating our two-year anniversary. He'd just proposed to me." She swallowed hard, trying to ignore the lump in her throat. "We came home, drank some wine, and danced barefoot in the living room."

"How much wine did you have?"

Chloe thought back. "One glass with dinner. Another when we got home."

"Were you drunk?"

She shook her head.

"Okay. You were dancing in the living room. Go on."

Chloe hesitated, reluctant to part with the last happy memories she had of the man she'd loved. "Michael and I went into the bedroom. That's when I saw him."

"Sylvio was in the bedroom?"

She nodded. "He was standing there with my gun."

"How'd you know it was your gun?"

"He said he'd found it in the nightstand drawer. Then he lectured me on gun safety and said I should've properly stored it in a lockbox."

"Okay." Dana took a breath. "What happened after that?"

Chloe felt her heartbeat pick up speed. "He told me to lie down on the bed beside Michael." She opened her mouth to say more, but nothing came out.

"Is that when he shot Michael?"

"I don't remember. The night stops there for me." She suspected a part of her did remember but was choosing to block it out. Every time she tried to push herself into remembering something more about that night, she felt her chest tighten like a boa constrictor was slowly draining the life from her.

"I haven't had a chance to read the case file yet," Dana said, "so I'm asking these questions blind. How much do you know about Michael's death? And if you're uncomfortable talking about this part, I under—"

"He was found in bed with a single gunshot wound to the head."

"Were there any other injuries?"

"Ligature marks on his wrists and ankles were the only injuries listed in the coroner's report. That's how he was found—tied to the bed with rock-climbing rope."

"So…Sylvio made you both lie on the bed." Dana frowned. "But he shot only one of you. Why do you think he wanted you on the bed if he wasn't going to shoot you?"

Chloe quickly surmised where Dana was going with this. "You think he raped me that night."

"I'm sitting here trying to think like a sadistic psychopath. There's no better way to humiliate a woman cop who gave me a speeding ticket than to rape her in front of her boyfriend. Killing the boyfriend with the cop's gun would really get me off. That would show her I'm the one who has all the power."

The minute the words were out of Dana's mouth, images, smells, and sounds from the past assaulted her senses. She heard Sylvio's voice clearly in her mind…*I'm the one in control now, Officer.* He'd spat the word *officer* with such hatred and rage. Chloe squeezed her eyes shut, willing her mind to slow down and give her only what she could handle.

Dana was still and silent as Chloe sifted through the horrors of that night. "He made me undress while he held the gun to Michael's head." She remembered the assault now as clearly as she remembered Sylvio's hands and voice. She had always known she was raped, from the medical report, but she had never been able to recall any of it until now. Beaten to a point where she was physically unrecognizable to anyone who knew her, she was comatose when she was found. Her doctor did a rape kit during that time only because it was obvious she'd been sexually assaulted. She'd had two years to wrap her head around the fact that her body had been violated in such a vile and despicable way. But knowing and remembering were two very different things, she realized. This way was a lot more painful.

"Sylvio was so angry. Beyond angry. He was enraged. I remember it now. He beat me and raped me that night." Chloe opened her eyes and looked at Dana. "He told us to say good-bye. Then he shot Michael in the head with my gun." She remembered the sound of her 9 mm as it betrayed her in Sylvio's hands—the hands she would forever remember.

Taz stood, put his head in her lap, and whined softly as tears spilled down her cheeks.

Dana got up from the sofa and walked around Taz to sit beside Chloe. "I'm so sorry about Michael...about what the two of you went through that night." She reached out, took Chloe's hand, and held it firmly between hers. "I'm sure there's a part of you that never wanted to remember what happened. Some would say your memory loss is a blessing, but it's not, Chloe. You owe it to yourself and to Michael to remember exactly what that son of a bitch did to you, so we can hold him accountable and put him away for good."

Still crying, Chloe nodded. She knew everything Dana said was true. This was all just part of the journey to getting justice for her and Michael. "I was going to say thanks for the push to remember, but I've decided not to." She squeezed Dana's hand and managed a small smile. "Because what I'd really be saying is...thanks for the push over the cliff into what feels like a dark and bottomless pit of anguish and despair."

Dana frowned. "I think I liked the first one better."

They finished their hot cocoa and decided to call it a night. Dana walked Chloe to the guest bedroom with Taz close behind.

Chloe was surprised to discover she didn't want to be alone, which she found curious because that was all she'd wanted for the last two years. Taz was there, she reminded herself. But it was human companionship she found herself craving. And not just anyone would do. She wanted Dana.

Was this newfound desire driven by fear, she wondered? Or was it prompted by the connection she felt with Dana? She wasn't sure. All she knew for certain was she didn't want Dana to leave. Chloe stepped into the guest room and sat on the bed. She considered asking Dana to stay but decided against it for fear of creating an awkward moment between them.

Dana lingered in the doorway. "Do you want me to sit with you for a while until you fall—"

"Yes," she blurted before Dana had even finished.

Dana went to a chair in one corner of the room and carried it to Chloe's bedside.

"Is it weird if I asked you to just…lie down with me?" Chloe asked, instantly regretting her words as she felt herself blush.

"Depends."

She looked up from the floor. "On what?"

"Do I have to compete with Taz for a spot on the bed? Something tells me I'd be on the losing end of that wrestling match." Dana raised one eyebrow at Taz, who was now standing in front of her and wagging his tail at the mention of his name.

Chloe laughed out loud, glad for a break in the tension. "Should be plenty of room," she said, scooting over on the bed. "He always sleeps beside me on the floor."

An automatic night-light blinked on in the corner as Dana clicked off the lamp and settled under the covers beside her. They both lay down and turned on their sides to face one another.

"You did great tonight," Dana whispered.

"So did you," Chloe whispered back.

"We'll get through this. I promise." Dana extended her hand, inviting Chloe to place hers inside.

Chloe smiled and reached back. "I know," she said, grateful for Dana's warm touch as she closed her eyes and dozed off.

❖

Dana watched Chloe's breathing deepen as she fell asleep. Still holding her hand, she studied her in the darkness. This woman captivated her. The strength it had taken for Chloe to survive what had happened and the courage it took to remember were unfathomable to Dana.

She and Maribel had done the right thing by extending their support. After all this time dealing with it alone, Chloe deserved to have someone on whom she could lean.

Her mind drifted to Gabbi, and—as it did—she withdrew her hand from Chloe's. There was little doubt in her mind that Sylvio had also abducted, assaulted, and murdered Gabbi. There were too many similarities between the two cases to be ignored.

It was hard to believe four years had passed since Gabriela's death. After all this time, it looked like she was finally going to get justice for her wife. She never would have found Sylvio without Chloe. Not a single shred of evidence—nothing whatsoever—had pointed in his direction.

She sat up in bed and looked around for Taz. He was sound asleep on the floor right beside Chloe. It was almost as if he sensed her vulnerability, too. Settling back underneath the covers, she replaced her hand over the top of Chloe's, closed her eyes, and started to drift. She promised herself she would call Maribel in the morning to share her thoughts on the case and compare notes.

CHAPTER SIX

Maribel picked up on the first ring.

"It's him," Dana said. "He's the one who took Gabbi." Chloe was in the shower, so there was no risk she'd overhear their conversation.

"I know. I reviewed Chloe's case file yesterday."

"We talked last night. She remembers what happened the night he took her."

"Good. I'll rearrange my schedule this morning. Meet me at my office at nine so I can get her sworn statement."

"What was the date of Chloe's abduction?" Dana asked, suddenly curious. "I forgot to ask her."

"Exactly two years after Gabbi. November twelfth."

Which demonstrated Sylvio's compulsive need to stick with a schedule. November twelfth obviously held significance for him. She wondered what it was. "What about the other two women?"

"I've compared the case files. Based on the information gathered when the victims were discovered, they could have been taken on precisely that day—November twelfth. Same MO. He's our guy."

Dana shook her head and sighed. "Four victims."

"That we know of," Maribel added. "I'd be willing to bet there are more."

Silence reigned as they both absorbed the reality behind those words.

"I can't believe we finally found the bastard," Dana said. After four long years, the moment felt surreal.

"Would've taken us a lot longer to find him. He sped things along for us by visiting Chloe at the station yesterday."

"I'll be sure to send him a thank-you from all of us at the BPD." Dana told her about their close call yesterday with the shooter at Chloe's condo. "When he dumped Chloe in front of her old department two years ago, I don't think he expected her to survive. All of his other victims died, and I'm pretty sure he'd planned it that way. He made a mistake with Chloe. Now he's trying to fix it."

"That's exactly what he's doing," Maribel agreed. "He's tying up loose ends. Without her, he knows we have no case." She paused. "But there's one thing I don't understand. Why'd he wait two years? He had all this time to kill her. Waiting that long substantially increases the risk of being caught. Doesn't make any sense."

Dana returned to her earlier thought. "It does if you're in Sylvio's mind. He's keeping to a schedule. For whatever reason, November twelfth holds significance for him."

"I wonder what it is. Think we'll ever find out?"

"I don't know," Dana admitted. "And frankly, I don't care. All I want right now is justice for the people he tortured and killed."

❖

Chloe smelled faint traces of Maribel's perfume as she stepped off the elevator. It was simultaneously sweet and sultry—like gardenias dipped in chardonnay. Dana led her down the corridor, greeted the receptionist, and poked her head inside Maribel's office. "Sorry we're late. There was an accident on Boylston."

Maribel ushered them in and closed the door behind them. "Dana already told me what happened yesterday. I'm glad you two are okay." Dressed in an elegant chocolate-brown pantsuit and ivory silk blouse, she walked around to the other side of her desk, pushed a button on the phone, and addressed the receptionist. "No interruptions please. Thanks, Andrew." She looked at Dana and then at Chloe, pointing to the two charcoal-gray wingback chairs that faced her desk. "Have a seat."

Dana slipped out of her jacket and hung it on the coatrack next to the door. Chloe sat and crossed her legs but decided to keep hers on. She wasn't sure if the chill in the air was real or imagined.

Maribel studied her as she took a seat behind the desk. "Dana says you recovered some memories last night."

Chloe nodded, looking around the office. "I remember the first night—the night he broke in to Michael's house." She'd been here dozens of times to consult with Maribel on different cases. Being on the other side of the desk felt like a shock to the system. "One down. Twenty-four to go," she said, knowing there were still twenty-four days unaccounted for in her mind. "I only remember bits and pieces of the other days—smells, sounds, fleeting images—but nothing concrete like the first night."

"Remembering that is huge progress, Chloe. We'll start there." Maribel withdrew a digital tape recorder from a drawer and set it in the middle of the desk. "Let's review that first night in as much detail as you can give me. Are you ready?" Maribel picked up the tape recorder, her finger poised over the button to record.

Chloe took a deep breath, reluctant to share the details of the horrors she'd faced. She wished Taz was here to lay his head in her lap.

"You can do this," Dana said from the chair beside her.

Chloe took them through everything, play by play. But when it came time to describe how Sylvio had violated her body, she froze. The words just wouldn't come.

Maribel paused the tape recorder.

"What's going on in your mind right now, Chloe?" Dana asked, scooting her chair closer.

It took her a few moments to identify what she was feeling because she had never felt it before. She felt a profound sense of *shame*. Even more disturbing was the realization that Michael had been forced to witness the entire assault. That was Michael's last image before he died. In that moment, she hated Sylvio more than she'd ever believed humanly possible. By sheer force of will, she decided to replace the shame with steadfast determination—just like she'd done throughout her life whenever she faced anything difficult. Besides, this shame wasn't hers. Sylvio was its rightful owner. The problem was he had no conscience. As a textbook example of a psychopath, he wasn't able to feel even the most basic of human emotions. But that wasn't her cross to bear. It was his.

Almost instantly, Chloe felt the warmth restored to her body. No longer cold, she stood, shrugged out of her coat, and hung it on the coatrack beside Dana's. "I'm okay," she said, returning to her chair. "Let's keep going."

Without shame or embarrassment, Chloe spoke about what had been done to her body. She shared every detail she could remember—down to the tattoo of a human skeleton in the center of Sylvio's chest. Finished, she looked up and searched Dana's face, wondering if everything she'd just shared would change the way Dana looked at her.

Dana reached out, took her hand, and gave it a gentle squeeze. She had tears in her eyes as she turned to Maribel. "She doesn't remember the rest of what happened yet. But that's enough to make an arrest."

"Damn right it is," Maribel said.

"What now?" Chloe asked.

Maribel crossed her arms. "We don't let you out of our sight."

"Until when? The trial?" Chloe asked jokingly.

Maribel and Dana exchanged a knowing glance.

"I was joking," Chloe said. "Because we all know that's months away." She looked back and forth between the two women. "Something's up. What aren't you telling me?"

Silence draped over the room like a shawl.

"There are other victims," Dana said finally.

Chloe felt sick to her stomach. "He's done this before?" It didn't surprise her. She'd always suspected she wasn't the first. For a sociopath like Sylvio, tormenting women would quickly become an art form. Still, the confirmation gave her no satisfaction. "How many?"

"Three that we know of. Four, including you." Maribel walked around her desk and sat on the edge, facing Chloe. "But we think there are more."

"Why wasn't he identified sooner? Why hasn't anyone testified against him?"

Maribel laced her fingers together in her lap. "None of the other victims survived."

"We haven't been able to link him to the other three women yet," Dana explained. "But the MO is nearly identical."

"How so?"

"For one, your injuries. The other women sustained injuries identical to yours, right down to the placement of the bite marks on their breasts."

The knowledge that three other women went through what she did and didn't make it was painful and disturbing on a very personal level. She now felt connected to those women in a way that was difficult to explain, even to herself. "Did he abduct them, too?"

Dana nodded. "Yes, and based on what we know, there's a high likelihood each woman was abducted on the same date— November twelfth. Looks like he kept each victim for the same amount of time—twenty-five days."

"What number was I?"

"You're the most recent," Dana said. "Number four. The previous one was two years before that."

Chloe's mind raced. She was abducted Saturday, November twelfth. That date was seared into her memory. "The two-year anniversary of my abduction was yesterday." Her stomach somersaulted. "Does he have a new victim?"

"Not from what we can tell. At least so far, no one's been reported missing," Dana assured her.

"We think that's why he showed up at the station yesterday. He has his eye on you again."

Chloe's instincts told her they were right. If she was the only one who survived, Sylvio was coming to finish his work. He had waited two long years. She shuddered to imagine what he had planned. "What else do the cases share? Lay it out for me."

Dana sighed. "You sure you want to know?"

She nodded.

"Each victim was abducted, kept for an extended period of time, intermittently beaten and sexually assaulted, and then left for dead in a conspicuous place."

That all rang true with Chloe. She didn't remember anything about it, but she knew from the police report that she was dumped in front of the Tisbury Police Department just after midnight. Her old partner had just started the graveyard shift. He was the one who'd found her. Sylvio had meticulously dressed her in her police uniform. If she hadn't been wearing that, no one at the station would have recognized her. Her injuries were too extensive.

"There's one more thing." Dana stood and walked to a window overlooking Downtown Boston. "You mentioned something last night about giving Sylvio a speeding ticket three weeks before he took you. I bet the women he targets have wronged him in some way—at least, that's the way *he* sees it."

Chloe narrowed her eyes. "How do you figure?"

Dana crossed her arms and looked out over the city. "Well, I can't say for sure, but I have a feeling that's what happened with Gabbi."

Chloe was so stunned she couldn't think of a thing to say. Her mind strained to put all the pieces together. Dana had said Gabbi was attacked in the parking lot where she worked four years ago. Two years before her. That would make Gabbi the third victim.

"After you told me about the speeding ticket, I remembered something Gabbi said before she disappeared. It seemed inconsequential at the time, so I never gave it a second thought... until this morning. Gabbi came home one night after her shift at the hospital. She mentioned this guy who showed up at the ER with a cut on his finger. He'd sliced it while cooking and needed stitches. She was in the middle of cleaning his wound when another emergency came in. She had to duck out for a little while. By the time she got back to him, he was gone. One of the other nurses on the floor saw him as he was leaving. He told her to tell Gabbi he didn't appreciate being made to wait." Dana turned from the window to focus on Chloe. "But the part that clinched it for me was hearing you talk about the tattoo on Sylvio's chest. The nurse who saw Gabbi's patient leave said his shirt was unbuttoned when he walked out, and there was a creepy skeleton tattoo in the middle of his chest."

Chloe stood and joined her by the window. She felt the keen sting of betrayal from Dana's blatant omission of this fact during their conversation last night. "Why didn't you tell me he killed Gabbi?"

"Because I wasn't sure of anything until now. We just started putting this all together yesterday."

She couldn't pull her eyes from Dana's. The bond they shared was clear to her now. Chloe had unwittingly become Gabbi's lifeline. Dana's only hope of getting justice for Gabbi rested squarely on Chloe's testimony. "You said the other victims were left for dead. Were they all alive when they were found?"

"Yes. But barely."

She started pacing, remembering what Dana had shared about staying in the ICU with Gabbi for three days before she died. "Most serial killers want to be there when the victim dies. But he gets off on the thrill of giving loved ones hope that the victim will actually pull through." She stopped pacing, looked to Dana and then to Maribel. "To him, I'm not just a loose end. I'm like an unfinished painting that was hung by mistake in the gallery. He's on a schedule for the ritualized abduction of women who've wronged him. His deep-seated compulsions won't allow him to deviate from that schedule, which explains why he hasn't come after me before now."

"Dana came to the same conclusion. That's why we're not letting you out of our sight." Maribel stood, walked around the desk, and sat back down in her chair.

Still mentally surfing her abductor's psychological profile, she returned to her chair and met Maribel's eyes. "Let me review the other case files. I can help."

"Absolutely not. You know as well as I do you're not allowed to aid in the investigation of your own case."

"But this is my area of expertise," Chloe pleaded.

"Your only job right now is to remember the other twenty-four days." Maribel turned to Dana. "And your job is to stay with her and do what you can to help her recover those memories. Neither of you can be involved in this case on an investigative level from here on out. You're both too close."

"Copy that." Dana gave Chloe a reassuring wink from across the room.

"I saw that," Maribel said, resting her elbows on the desk and throwing them both a stern look. "I mean it, Dana. Do *not* jeopardize my case."

Chapter Seven

B ack at Dana's, they made sandwiches together in the kitchen. Chloe was just opening a bag of chips when her cell phone rang. She put it on speaker.

"Sylvio's in custody," Maribel said on the other end of the line.

Chloe felt ice cold fingers travel the length of her spine.

"Arraignment and bail hearing are set for tomorrow at ten. I'll push like hell to get bail denied. Like I said, though, no guarantees."

"We'll keep our fingers crossed," Dana said, brushing against Chloe's shoulder as she leaned on the counter beside her.

If bail was granted—even with Taz and Dana by her side— Chloe didn't know how she'd sleep at night.

"In the meantime, keep chipping away at those memories. All we have right now is your word against his, Chloe. I need more to work with here."

Dana straightened. "The nurse I was telling you about—at the hospital where Gabbi worked. Did you find her?"

"Still working on that. I'll keep you posted."

They ended the call and sat at the kitchen table to eat. Chloe didn't have much of an appetite. Judging from the way she was staring at her uneaten sandwich, neither did Dana. They both looked up from their plates.

"Let's go for a run," Dana suggested. "There's a great trail not far from here."

"You read my mind." Chloe breathed a sigh of relief. "Can Taz come?"

Dana looked across the kitchen at Taz, who was waiting patiently for Chloe to take her first bite so he could eat. A turkey sandwich, minus the bread, was on the menu for him today. "Will you be the one to break it to him?" Dana asked.

"Break what to him?"

"That we're not actually going to eat as originally planned. Dogs shouldn't run on a full stomach, right?"

"Trust me, that won't be a problem." She stood from the table without taking a bite of her sandwich. "Taz, do you want to go for a run?"

Tail wagging at full speed, he leaped up and pranced in place.

"Go get your leash," she said.

When Taz cocked his head to one side and looked at her, she pointed in the direction of the guest room. "It's on the bed," she reminded him.

He tore off at a gallop down the hall and around the corner, his lunch all but forgotten. Chloe retrieved the turkey and put it in the fridge for later.

"That's amazing," Dana said, craning her neck to peer down the hall. "Is he really going to get his—"

Taz sprinted back and slid into a sit on the tile in front of Chloe, the reflective red leash dangling from his mouth.

"He's so smart I'm beginning to think Maribel should consult with him on this case," Dana said. "I'll go change into my workout clothes."

They drove to a trailhead twenty minutes away. Dana put her SUV in park, withdrew an extra clip of bullets from the glove compartment, and zipped them inside the pocket of her CamelBak. She adjusted her shoulder harness underneath a black Nike running shirt and looked at Chloe. "Ready when you are."

Chloe took it easy on her for the first mile, but Dana didn't even break a sweat. She picked up the pace gradually over the next fifteen minutes until she was running her normal seven-minute mile. Dana kept up with no problem.

"You're fast," Chloe finally conceded.

"Running has always been one of the ways I relieve stress."

"Me, too," Chloe admitted. "What are some of the others?"

Dana glanced at her. "What do you mean?"

"The other ways you relieve stress. What are they?"

"Well, I only have two." Dana seemed uncomfortable all of a sudden. "And one of them I haven't done in a while."

Chloe took a sip from her CamelBak, waiting.

"Okay. I'll say it...sex."

"That used to be mine, too," Chloe said, breaking the tension as they both laughed.

"My turn," Dana said, glancing over with a wry grin. "You mentioned last night you were with a woman before."

"Forget about that. I was half drunk and afraid you thought I was homophobic."

"So you lied?"

"I dated a girl my junior and senior years of college."

"Just one girl?"

Chloe nodded. "I was madly in love with her."

"What happened?"

"She cheated on me, broke my heart. I swore off all women after that." Chloe slowed to a stop, unzipped Taz's collapsible bowl, and filled it with water from her CamelBak. He lapped away happily. "No one since Gabbi?" Chloe asked.

Dana shook her head.

"How come?"

Dana was suddenly quiet.

Taz put a paw on the side of his bowl to drain the remaining water, picked it up with his front teeth, and handed it to Chloe.

"Are you sure there's not a person in there pretending to be a dog?"

"Sometimes I wonder the same." Chloe folded the bowl in half, zipped it up, and clipped it to her CamelBak.

Dana was still staring at Taz. "I'm pretty sure he would've done that for you if he had opposable thumbs."

"This is a nice trail," Chloe said, mindful of steering the conversation to safer terrain. "Thanks for taking me here." She checked her watch, surprised to discover they'd already covered four miles.

"It's a six-mile loop. The last two are my favorite," Dana said, setting off again.

They covered the last two miles in silence, easing their strides to take in the scenery. Fifty degree weather and clear skies made for the perfect run. The afternoon sun illuminated the forest around them, enhancing an already spectacular display of color. At the tail-end of autumn, many trees had already shed their leaves. But there were more than a few stragglers that held on to their brightly colored foliage later than the others, perhaps hoping to bedazzle passersby with less competition from their sleepy, bare-branched neighbors.

Leaves crunched underfoot as they ran. Ravens crowed from the vanishing canopy above. The natural aromas of trees, dried leaves, and moist earth were intoxicating. For the first time in a long time, Chloe felt glad to be alive.

They finished the loop, drank some water, and piled inside Dana's SUV. Chloe was starving. "*Now* I'm hungry."

Taz chuffed in agreement from the back seat.

"I swear his grasp of the English language is better than mine," Dana said, pulling out of the dirt lot.

"Can we stop at the store? I'm craving Ben and Jerry's."

"What kind?"

"New York Super Fudge Chunk."

"You're kidding. I happen to have two unopened pints of that in my freezer downstairs."

"Perfect." Chloe was already looking forward to dessert.

Dana glanced over uncertainly. "Unless…"

"Unless what?"

"Will Taz require his own pint?"

Chloe shook her head. "I know it's hard to believe, but he doesn't like ice cream."

"All dogs like ice cream."

"It makes him sneeze."

"He's allergic to ice cream?"

Chloe looked out the window as they made their way to paved roads again.

"I didn't know how to answer the question you asked earlier," Dana said.

"About why there hasn't been anyone since Gabbi?"

She nodded.

"You don't have to answer that. It's none of my business."

"I wanted to answer. I just didn't want to give you the answer I tell everyone else."

"Which is what?" Chloe asked, her curiosity piqued.

"That I'm not ready."

"Not being ready after what happened to Gabbi is a very valid answer. There's no need to come up with anything better."

"That was the truth for the first two years," Dana admitted.

"And the last two?"

"I couldn't let myself move forward until I found the bastard who hurt her. That's the closure I need," Dana said, gripping the steering wheel tightly. "That's the closure Gabbi deserves."

❖

Chloe jogged up the courthouse steps, paused outside the enormous wooden double doors, and slid her hands inside her coat pockets. The last few steps might as well have been twenty miles. She stepped aside to let several people pass.

Dana came up beside her and leaned against the building. "You don't have to do this."

"Yes, I do." She turned to face Dana. "He's not expecting me to be here today. I need to go in there and show him…" She shivered at the thought of what it would feel like to see him again. Maybe she wasn't ready to do this. Her stomach felt like Jell-O.

"Show him what, Chloe?"

What had she hoped to accomplish by attending Sylvio's arraignment? Suddenly, the idea seemed ludicrous. But then she remembered the bastard's intimidating smirk when she'd locked eyes with him at the station a few days ago. She withdrew her hands from her pockets, opened the courthouse door, and looked back over her shoulder at Dana. "I need to go in there and show him I'm not afraid."

"Fair enough," Dana said, close on her heels. "But I won't be giving you CPR a second time around."

They approached the security checkpoint as Chloe took her place in line. "Would giving me mouth-to-mouth really be that unpleasant for you?" she teased.

"No," Dana retorted, playfully cutting in her line. "Which is exactly why I won't be doing it again." She set her overcoat on the X-ray belt, held up her badge, and identified herself to the court officer. "Detective Blake, Boston Police." She unbuttoned her blazer to show him she was armed. "I'm escorting this witness, Dr. Chloe Maddox, who's also a BPD police officer."

Chloe held out her badge. She didn't bother showing him her gun. She didn't have one. They'd talked about it last night and decided it was a bad idea for her to be armed on a day like today.

The potbellied court officer paid little attention to their badges. "Oh, yeah, Detective Blake," he said, directing his eyes at her breasts as he spoke. "You work with my cousin, Harry."

"Forgive me"—Dana made a point of reading his badge—"Officer Lepene, but I can't seem to find it."

He finally looked up from her breasts, his greasy forehead riddled with pimples and stupidity. "Find what?"

"Well, since you're doing me the favor of staring at my breasts, I'd like to return the favor by staring at your penis." She stepped back and let her eyes drop. "Problem is, I can't find it," she said, squinting.

"Listen here, *Detective*," he said, his face contorting into an unpleasant grimace. "This is *my* house—"

"And that's my house." Dana pointed out the window directly behind him. "Not just a courthouse. All of Boston. So think real hard before you finish that sentence. Life can be tough out there, Officer Lepene. And if you think Harry's gonna help you out of this one just because you're family, think again. Harry and I go way back." She winked. "If you know what I mean."

He opened his mouth to say something but thought better of it and waved them through without another word. As they walked away, Chloe felt his eyes burning holes in her backside until they rounded the corner.

She looked at Dana, unable to hide the admiration in her voice. "So *that's* how you command respect from your peers. Witty retorts, intimidation, and general abuse of power."

"The best part is I have an unlimited arsenal of witty retorts. I thought the penis one up a few weeks ago. I've been dying for the chance to use it."

Maribel stopped them on their way into the courtroom. "What are you two doing here?" she asked, stepping aside. Without waiting for an answer, she turned to Chloe. "You're not required to be here today. It's just the arraignment."

"I know," Chloe said. "I'm here because I want to be."

The ADA looked to Dana, who just shrugged and resumed scanning passersby. Dana was like her own personal bodyguard, never letting Chloe move more than a couple of feet from her.

Maribel frowned. "I don't like this."

"She's okay," Dana said. "And I'll be with her the whole time."

Chloe glanced at her watch: 9:56 a.m. "Judges don't like tardy prosecutors."

"She armed?"

Dana brought a hand to the gun at her hip. "No."

"Are you sure?"

Dana blinked. "Pretty."

"For God's sake, I'm right here." Chloe sighed. "I can hear you. And no, I'm not armed."

Maribel grabbed her by the elbow and led her to a room a few doors down. She knocked on the door. When no one answered, she opened it and pushed Chloe inside. Dana followed.

"If you have a weapon on you, I need to know now. I can't risk you taking justice into your own hands today, Chloe."

She felt her anger rising to the surface, but the cop in her understood. Maribel's concerns were justified. She slipped out of her coat, lifted her shirt away from her body, and turned in a slow circle. "See? No weapon."

"I need to be sure."

"Aside from strip-searching me, I guess you'll just have to take me at my word."

"You'll consent to a pat-down if you plan on coming into that courtroom with me." Maribel checked her watch and tapped her high-heeled foot.

Chloe turned her eyes on Dana and nodded.

Dana moved around behind her and tugged on the sleeve of her blazer. "Can you take this off?"

She did, feeling more than a little vulnerable with the detective at her back. She braced herself for the first touch, but when Dana's hands found her, she couldn't stop her body from responding to the threat by pulling away. "Sorry." She spun around. "I'd rather you do this facing me, where I can see you."

Dana nodded and stepped forward. She ran firm hands along Chloe's shoulders, down her arms, over each hip, down the inside of one leg and then the other. She straightened and moved closer, slipping her arms underneath Chloe's to run her hands along the length of her back and buttocks. Heat radiated from Dana's body as she pressed up against her.

Finished, she pulled back. Their eyes locked. Chloe realized they were both breathing a little faster.

"She's clean," Dana said, never taking her eyes from Chloe's.

"Couldn't she be hiding a weapon in her bra?"

"She's not." Dana swallowed hard and let her gaze drop. "I'd have felt it."

CHAPTER EIGHT

Maribel led them into the courtroom and gestured to the empty bench directly behind the prosecution. Sylvio was nowhere in sight. Chloe took a seat and draped her coat over the back of the bench, her eyes glued to the defense attorney across the room. His Ken-doll hair, Rolex watch, and custom-made suit hinted at high-priced success.

Quick intelligent eyes darted to Maribel as he nodded a tight-lipped greeting. He looked immediately to Chloe and then to Dana, giving her a curt, begrudging nod before unlatching and flipping open his briefcase.

Chloe leaned toward Dana. "You two know each other?" she whispered.

Dana slid an arm behind her and set it across the top of the bench. "That's Chris Slater. He asked me out a few times, back when he was an ADA."

"He was a prosecutor?" she asked, unable to fathom how someone could switch to the other side of the law.

"One of the best. But there was always something about him that didn't sit right with me."

A door near the front of the courtroom swung open. Two prison guards led Sylvio to his attorney. Handcuffed, he was impeccably dressed in a light gray Armani suit, white shirt, red tie, and black leather shoes that probably cost more than Chloe's entire wardrobe.

Chris pulled out a chair as one of the guards unlocked Sylvio's cuffs. They exchanged pleasantries, shook hands, and took their seats. Sylvio suddenly stiffened. He turned his head slowly in Chloe's direction. Stone gray eyes centered on hers.

Chloe fought to keep her breakfast down. She knew that look all too well. Her heart hammered against her ribcage as she met his gaze, unrelenting in her determination to make him pay for what he did.

Dana reached over to take Chloe's hand and simultaneously flipped Sylvio the bird. This unexpected and blatantly juvenile gesture made Chloe laugh out loud. She watched Sylvio's eyes harden with fury as he turned away and whispered something in his attorney's ear.

"Rat bastard," Dana whispered. "Look at his tie."

Chloe studied Sylvio's red tie more closely. It was covered with images of tiny German shepherds—his way of telling her he knew about Taz. Which could mean only one thing: he'd been watching her.

The bailiff strode into the courtroom. "All rise. The Honorable Samuel Brown presiding. Court is now in session."

Everyone stood as the judge ascended the steps to the bench. The bailiff told everyone to be seated as Judge Brown peered over his bifocals at Maribel. "Fill me in, Ms. Murphy."

Maribel cited the charges and asked that bail be denied on the grounds that the defendant was responsible for the recent attempt on Chloe's life.

"Mr. Slater, how does your client plead?"

Chris replied, "Your Honor, my client pleads not guilty to all charges. And we request that he be released on his own recognizance. I won't waste the Court's time addressing the allegation that my client tried to murder the alleged victim in this case. Because he did no such thing. And ADA Murphy has zero proof to the contrary. As to the rape charges, my client does not refute the fact that he and Dr. Maddox were intimate." Chris glanced in Maribel's direction with an arrogant smirk. "But he didn't rape her. He didn't have to. In fact, we have irrefutable proof that what occurred between my client and Dr. Maddox was purely consensual."

Judge Brown removed his bifocals and proceeded to wipe them with a handkerchief. "And what proof is that, Mr. Slater?"

"We have a DVD, Your Honor."

Maribel turned and raised a questioning eyebrow at Chloe, but Chloe just shook her head. She had no idea what he was talking about.

"Care to elaborate, Mr. Slater?" The judge scowled. "Or would you prefer to keep us on the edge of our seats until trial?"

"Forgive me, Your Honor." He opened a folder, withdrew a clear plastic case containing the DVD, and waved it in the air. "This disk proves Dr. Maddox had sexual intercourse with my client." He turned his head and let his eyes roam knowingly over Chloe's body. "*Consensual* sexual intercourse," he added.

The courtroom swam in and out of focus. Chloe felt her world turning upside down. For a split second, she fantasized about grabbing Dana's gun, shooting the bastard's balls off, and holding them up to the judge as evidence he didn't have any.

Maribel leaned over and kept her voice down. "Do you know anything about this disk?"

Not trusting herself to speak, Chloe shook her head.

Maribel straightened. "Your Honor, Dr. Maddox has no knowledge of the disk in question—"

"And I have a signed affidavit saying she does." Chris pulled out a sheet of paper and handed it to the bailiff, who then walked it over to Maribel.

"Not only did she consent to being videotaped, but she also consented to the distribution of the film at my client's sole discretion. I'd be happy to pass along a copy of this video to the prosecution for review."

The judge peered over his bifocals. "Well, Ms. Murphy, it looks like Mr. Slater is in a generous mood this morning. Do you find his offer acceptable?"

"Yes, Your Honor."

"Very well. Prosecution will review the disk, and we'll reconvene at nine tomorrow. Bail hearing is adjourned until then." Judge Brown lifted his gavel and slammed it against the wooden block.

❖

Chloe paced in front of Maribel's office door and checked her watch for the twentieth time. She felt queasy, lightheaded. Dana had driven her there straight from the courthouse. They'd been waiting for over an hour. *Oh God, if Maribel doesn't get here soon...* She was losing her grip by the second.

Ding. The elevator doors parted down the hall. Dana stood and peered around the corner. "Here she comes."

Maribel strode past without even glancing in Chloe's direction. She unlocked her office door, shrugged out of a long olive-green overcoat, and hung it on the rack. "Shut the door, please," she said, setting her briefcase on the desk.

Chloe knew immediately something had changed. Maribel was avoiding eye contact. Feeling more uneasy by the second, she stood in front of the desk. "Please don't tell me you watched the video."

"I had to. It was evidence." Maribel transferred several files from her briefcase to her desk and finally looked up. "I'm sorry."

Chloe could see the regret in Maribel's eyes. "Okay. I need to see it," she said sadly.

Without another word, Maribel handed her the disk.

Chloe slid it into the DVD player on the TV in the corner, hesitated, and finally hit *play.* Dana leaned against the desk beside her, their shoulders touching.

The screen went black for the first few seconds until a bedroom came into view. The camera zoomed in on a metal canopy bed. Two matching nightstands stood on either side, their surfaces dotted with flickering white candles. Romantic notes from a saxophone massaged the quiet space. Chloe stood beside the bed in a red negligee, donning black fishnet stockings, black fishnet gloves that ended just above her elbows, and red spiked high heels.

Sylvio sauntered into the room in khakis and a royal blue long-sleeved button-down. She remembered his smell perfectly—a cologne she'd later identified as Issey Miyake's L'Eau Bleue. Traces of earth, wood, and spice combined to give him his signature aroma. She smelled it just as strongly now as if he was standing there in the room beside her.

Carrying a single red rose, he walked over and held it out to her. She accepted it. Her body language was relaxed, as well it should be after polishing off an entire bottle of white zinfandel single-handedly. She remembered this now. She'd convinced him to let her get drunk in order to give him a better performance.

She set the rose on the nightstand and went to him, unbuttoning his shirt, loosening his belt, unzipping his fly. He caressed her through the silky fabric of the negligee while she reached into his pants to stroke him. Still wearing the fishnet stockings and gloves, she pulled away, kicked off her heels, and eased back onto the bed. Not once did their lips touch. She had no idea why, but kissing was off-limits to Sylvio. It was the one loving act she'd managed to keep sacred.

Staged to look like homemade porn, the video left little to the imagination. Chloe was frozen in place, embarrassed beyond measure, and sick to her stomach.

Dana stepped to the side of the TV and pressed *pause*. "He was trying to hide the ligature marks on your wrists and ankles with the fishnet." She pointed to three different places on the screen. "There...there...and there. It's hard to make out the bruising, but I can definitely see it." She turned to Maribel. "If we send this to the lab, they'll be able to give us a clearer picture and analysis of the ligature marks."

Chloe stood there, shocked. A few days ago, she'd had a simple and professional relationship with Dana and Maribel, both of whom had just gotten a very intimate glimpse into her private nightmare.

Deciding to follow Dana's lead, Chloe fast-forwarded the video and paused it. She tried to distance herself from the image, pretending as though it wasn't her body on the screen. "There's also bruising on the interior of my thighs. And see there?" She pointed to the screen. "Both the labia minora and labia majora are raw, bruised, and swollen from previous assaults. Any medical expert could analyze this and tell you"—it took her a minute, but she finally managed to swallow the sob at the back of her throat—"how much physical pain I endured during this video."

Maribel came up beside her and stared at the screen. "You remember this now?"

"I remember agreeing to this after he threatened me with things that were much, much worse." She met Maribel's haunted gaze. "This was the lesser of two evils."

They left Maribel's office, rode the elevator in silence, and walked through the garage to Dana's car. "I need to stop at my place to pick up a few things," Chloe said, shivering.

Dana nodded and slid the key in the ignition. She turned the heater on high and watched Chloe from the driver's seat. After seeing the video of her own assault, she could only imagine what Chloe was going through right now.

"Having to sit here with you after watching my Hollywood debut is pure torture. No offense, but I'd prefer never to see you again for as long as I live." Chloe sighed and gazed out the window. "Or for the next ten lifetimes if I happen to have the misfortune of being reincarnated."

Hearing the vulnerability in Chloe's voice, Dana remained quiet. She struggled to find something meaningful to say. "I farted once during my annual pap test."

Chloe stared at her.

"Loudly," Dana added. "The doc excused herself and returned with a surgical mask and a can of air freshener."

"You win on the humiliation scale." Chloe rolled her eyes. "Hands down."

"Would it help if I showed you one of my own sex tapes?" Dana asked.

Chloe sat up a little and looked over, a ray of hope unfolding in her face. "That actually might make me feel better."

"I was never brave enough to make one. But I do have some topless photos from spring break in college I'd be happy to share."

Chloe looked away. "He's been watching me," she said sadly. "How else would he know about Taz?"

She had no doubt Chloe was right. The tie was obviously meant to intimidate her. "Has anything else come back to you?"

"I remember that room. There were no windows, and it was cold most of the time. Felt like I was underground in a basement somewhere. It smelled like fresh paint and new carpet. I remember thinking it was newly built. But now I'm wondering if he threw in new carpet and a fresh coat of paint on the walls between victims." She turned to Dana with a look of profound sadness. "I bet he took us all to the same place."

The thought of Gabbi being kept in that room against her will and assaulted by that psycho made Dana want to saw off his penis, shove it where the sun didn't shine, and make him relive that moment over and over—like Bill Murray in the movie *Groundhog Day*.

Chloe withdrew her cell phone and started dialing.

"Who are you calling?" Dana asked.

Chloe put it on speaker as Maribel's voice came on the line in greeting. "If Sylvio videotaped me, he probably videotaped the other women, too. We need to get a search warrant and—"

"Already on it. Is Dana there with you?"

"I'm here," she said, pulling into the driveway of Chloe's condo.

"Sylvio's primary residence is on Martha's Vineyard," Maribel explained. "I'm now working in tandem with the Tisbury PD and the district attorney's office there. In fact, I just got off the phone with the DA. He's getting a search warrant as we speak and has agreed to give me access to the evidence as it pertains to this case. Get this," she said, a mixture of anger and disbelief in her voice. "Sylvio bought some condos in Wellesley just four days after you moved here."

"Close to my condo?" Chloe asked.

"The son of a bitch bought the entire complex, Chloe. Yours included."

CHAPTER NINE

Chloe couldn't care less if there was an assassin waiting to ambush her inside her condo. She had her mind on one thing. Part of her already knew what she'd find as she ducked underneath the yellow crime scene tape. She was heading toward the spiral staircase that led to the second floor when Dana caught up with her.

"Where are you going?"

Not trusting herself to speak, Chloe jogged up the stairs, marched into the bedroom, and stood in the middle of the room. She turned in a slow circle.

"What's going on, Chloe?"

She went to the TV near the foot of her bed and disconnected the cable modem. Dana looked over her shoulder as she pulled out the wireless video feed.

"Jesus Christ, Chloe."

She walked to the bathroom, pushed the shower curtain aside, and grabbed the waterproof CD player off the shelf. She smashed it against the tub a few times, cracking it open like a walnut. Dana watched her from the doorway as she sifted through the electronic components until she found a second wireless video feed. She knelt there, stunned.

"I'll call the guys and get an electronics team in here to do a sweep," Dana said, reaching for her cell.

Chloe stormed out of the bathroom. She picked up the nearest object and hurled it as hard as she could against the vanity mirror. The glass exploded and rained down around her—the sound of destruction satisfying to her ears. She went to the TV next, tore it out of the cubbyhole, and heaved it across the room. Then she grabbed everything she could find, anything within reach.

She ripped pictures off the walls and crushed them underfoot, slid drawers from the bureau and cracked them against the wall. Splintered pieces of wood were still flying through the air as she shattered a glass lamp against the headboard. Shards rebounded, grazing her face and neck.

Dana grabbed her arms from behind, brought her to the floor, and held her there.

Chloe twisted, bucked, kicked, and tried her damnedest to break free, but the more she fought, the harder Dana restrained her and kept her in place. "Easy," Dana whispered.

She was out of breath. "Let...me...go!"

"Not until you calm down."

She didn't have the strength to fight anymore. "He's been... watching me," she panted.

Dana eased up as Chloe's breathing slowed. "I know. I'm sorry." Dana stayed behind her and kept holding her as they sat together on the floor in silence.

Chloe was sure they'd find more hidden cameras in the condo. With Taz by her side and a state-of-the-art security system, she had believed she was safe. Her private sanctuary for the past year had been violated. Daily showers, getting dressed in the morning for work and undressed at the end of each day—he'd watched it all. And to think she came here a year ago to hunker down, lick her wounds, and move on with her life as best she could.

This whole time she had believed she was safe. Yet there he was, watching her every move. A witness in her struggle to remember him.

"I wish there was something I could do to make this better." Dana finally released her grip, turned Chloe around, and hugged her.

Chloe stiffened, unaccustomed to being hugged. But something about the way Dana held her made her guard come down. Dana's touch was strong and gentle at the same time. The feel of Dana's skin against her face was warm and reassuring. Before she had time to change her mind, she leaned into Dana and grabbed hold of her like a lifeline, shedding the pain and anger through tears that just wouldn't stop.

Dana couldn't believe the balls Sylvio had to break into a police officer's home to install surveillance equipment. He showed absolutely no fear of getting caught. A raging narcissistic ego clearly prevented him from even fathoming the possibility of getting caught. In his eyes, he was entitled to do what he did because Chloe was his.

Her heart went out to Chloe. She didn't know what she could say to make any of this okay. Aside from serving her Sylvio's head on a platter, there probably wasn't much anyone could do for her right now. Chloe was understandably pissed off. Being monitored in your own home took the feeling of violation to a whole new level. Losing her temper and destroying her own house showed a hell of a lot more self-control than Dana would've had in a similar position. Had it been her, she'd be on her way to his house right now...to ring the doorbell and blast his brains out the moment he opened the door.

She sat on the floor and held Chloe as tight as she dared. In that moment, Dana knew she would do whatever was necessary to protect her. Sylvio could never be allowed to hurt her again, physically or otherwise. If the court system failed them, Dana made a silent vow to take justice into her own hands and do what needed to be done.

❖

The electronics team found eleven different wireless video feeds cleverly camouflaged in different nooks and crannies throughout the condo, as well as one inside the empty cigarette lighter of Chloe's car.

Detective Ajay Stevens sidled over with the last of the paperwork and flashed his charismatic smile. He'd worked undercover narcotics for years before transferring to computer crimes, but he still had that bad-boy-in-a-rock-band look about him. And he carried it off pretty well, Chloe decided.

"Whoever did this is one sick bastard," he said, handing Chloe a pen for her signature. "But he sure has skills when it comes to surveillance. Maybe we should consider offering this guy a job."

She finished signing and handed the pen back. Neither she nor Dana laughed.

"My bad." Stevens raised the brim of his Red Sox ball cap. "Just trying to lighten the mood a little." He hooked his thumbs in the belt loops of his jeans and turned to Dana. "Guys are packed and ready to go as soon as they check your vehicle. Meet you at your place in twenty."

Dana nodded. "Thanks, Stevens. I'd appreciate if you and your team kept this to yourselves."

"Mum's the word," he said, turning to leave.

"Might be a little while until we get back here," Dana said. "Anything you want to take with you?"

Chloe shook her head. There was nothing at all she wanted from this place. In fact, she wanted to set everything in here on fire. Maybe detonate a few nuclear bombs while she was at it. It took every ounce of willpower not to do just that. She turned and walked out the front door without looking back.

After the SUV was declared free of surveillance devices, they climbed inside and headed to Dana's, where the team would do a precautionary sweep for more cameras. Fat snowflakes danced on the windshield and were quickly swept aside by the wipers. Snow had decided to make its first appearance early this year—a silver lining to an ugly day. At least the snow was pretty, Chloe thought.

They pulled into Dana's driveway twenty minutes later as the team was unloading their equipment from a white van.

"This shouldn't take long," she said to Chloe. "I don't expect they'll find anything."

Chloe blinked the snow from her eyes and hugged her coat closer to her body. She was anxious to see Taz and make sure he was okay.

Dana unlocked the door. They both stepped inside. Taz was perched a few feet away on the area rug—tail wagging, his entire body brimming with excitement at their reunion. He remained seated, patiently waiting for Chloe to unzip her coat and hang it up so he could give her a proper greeting.

"Is he baring his teeth at us?" Dana asked, watching as Chloe leaned over to let Taz give her a kiss on the nose.

"He's smiling. It means he's happy to see us."

"Of course. Taz smiles. What was I thinking?"

"Will you get over here and tell him you're happy to see him, too?"

Dana hung her coat in the closet and turned to face Taz. "It's true. I'm officially a fan," she said, reaching out to stroke his neck and shoulders. She looked at Chloe. "Hot cocoa?"

Dana led the way into the kitchen, put the kettle on the stove, and grabbed two mugs from the shelf above the sink. Chloe told Taz to lie down and stay as the team scanned Dana's house for wireless cameras.

Stevens joined them a short time later and gave them the thumbs-up. "All clear," he said, eyeballing Taz from afar. "I'll get to work on that trace and let you know as soon as I find something."

"How long?" Dana asked.

Stevens shrugged. "We should have something for you inside twenty-four hours." He couldn't take his eyes off Taz. "Hey, isn't that the crazy shepherd who got kicked out of K-9 school?"

Chloe watched as Taz lifted his head from his paws and pierced Stevens with a predatory gaze.

Dana shook her head and sighed. "I wouldn't talk about him like that if I were you."

"My brother was his handler," Stevens went on. "He always said that dog's crazier than a shoeshine in a shit storm."

Taz growled from his position on the floor.

Chloe went to Taz and knelt beside him, giving Stevens a look of warning. "No more insults unless you want me to start hurling them at your brother."

"There's nothing you could hurl that I haven't already hurled myself," Stevens said. "My brother's kind of an ass-head."

"You mean, asshole?" Chloe corrected.

"Ass-head," Stevens repeated. "He's always got his head up his ass, so that's what I call him." He walked over to Taz and reached out. "Sorry you got the ass-head as your handler, bud."

Chloe held her breath, fully expecting Stevens to have one less finger with which to continue his work in computer crimes. But Taz surprised her by giving his hand a little lick. Apparently, he was quick to forgive Stevens's familial relationship to the ass-head.

"He looks good," Stevens said, nodding. "Happy. He was never happy like this when I saw him. I'm glad he has a good home now."

Without another word, Stevens and the rest of his team left. The house grew quiet once more.

Chloe took Taz to the backyard for a potty run and then retreated to the guest room. It was two twenty p.m. Hard to believe she was only halfway through the day. She collapsed on the bed, feeling totally and utterly depleted.

Dressed in gray ski pants and a purple long-sleeved Nike shirt, Dana poked her head in and glanced at her watch. "We have about two hours of daylight left. Let's go for a hike."

Chloe got up, went to the window, and pulled the curtain aside. "In the snow?"

Dana tossed her a pair of ski pants identical to the ones she was wearing and disappeared around the corner.

She looked down at the pants and couldn't help but wonder if they were Dana's or Gabbi's. Was hiking something they'd done together as a couple? Her curiosity piqued, she changed and met Dana in the living room.

Snowshoes and ski poles were lined up near the front door. "What size shoe do you wear?" Dana asked.

"Eight."

She pointed to a pair of Columbia boots on the floor. "Those should fit you." They packed everything in the back of the SUV and climbed inside.

They drove the first few minutes in silence until Chloe spotted a photograph poking out from Dana's visor. "Is that Gabbi?" she asked.

Dana looked up and nodded, sliding the photo out to hand it to her. "From our day at the beach the summer before she was taken."

Gabbi was smiling at the camera, her honey-brown eyes full of laughter. Tan and lithe, she was ankle deep in foamy ocean waves. Her thumbs were hooked in the pockets of her white shorts, and her yellow tank top dipped off one shoulder to expose the graceful curve of collarbone and neck. She was so beautiful and full of life.

"You still miss her," Chloe said, unable to tear her eyes from the photo.

"I'll never stop. Sometimes I still can't believe she's gone."

Chloe could relate. She felt the same about Michael.

"Nobody knows this, but I was pregnant when Gabbi went missing."

Chloe looked up.

"Gabbi and I had talked about starting a family and decided it was time. We went to a fertility clinic. I'd have the first baby, and she would have the second a few years later." Dana smiled sadly. "As luck would have it, we were successful on the first try."

Chloe set the photo in her lap, silent as she waited for Dana to go on.

"I'll never forget how excited she was when I told her. She found another nurse to cover the rest of her shift at the hospital and came home with about a dozen different baby books."

Chloe already knew the answer but was afraid to ask. "What happened?"

"I was five weeks along when Gabbi disappeared." She glanced at Chloe. "I lost the baby the day after she died."

"I'm so sorry." She reached over and squeezed Dana's hand.

"It took me a long time to come to terms with losing our baby. I finally realized it just wasn't meant to be."

"Michael and I wanted kids, too," she confided. "We were planning to start trying as soon as we were married. Neither of us wanted to wait."

They fell silent for the last few minutes of the drive. Chloe looked down at their intertwined hands, thoughts of the past intersecting with thoughts of the future. Holding Dana's hand as they shared stories about their loved ones should have been awkward. But it wasn't. With this simple gesture, Chloe realized they were starting to move on. And moving on didn't mean they had to leave Gabbi or Michael behind.

They reached the trailhead, unpacked, and geared up. Taz hopped down from the car, unfazed by the snow-covered ground and eager for the hike to begin.

Chloe had never been snowshoeing before, but it was easy to learn. Her breath plumed from her mouth as they ascended the first hill. When the trail grew too narrow, they hiked single file with Taz between them. Dana quickened the pace. Neither of them made an attempt at conversation. They were breathing too hard to talk.

She shook her head and smiled to herself. Dana seemed to know *exactly* what she needed. Chloe was pushing her body so hard she didn't have the energy to think about anything else.

By the time they made it back to the parking lot, it had stopped snowing. Dusk was fully upon them. For the first time since they'd arrived, Chloe took a look around. Tall, furry pines stood guard, cloaked in their wintry white uniforms. Oak, birch, and maple trees had reached out to gather the snow with their branches. The effect was surreal, casting a peaceful wintry glow all around them.

Taz was panting heavily as Chloe unzipped his collapsible bowl and filled it with water. She sat beside Dana in the rear of the SUV until she felt her breathing and heart rate return to normal. Soaked in sweat from head to toe, she felt cleansed by the workout and invigorated by the cold. "What made you decide to be a cop?" she asked, breaking the long silence.

"My usual answer to that question is I never saw myself doing anything else."

Chloe pulled the hat from her head and smoothed out her curls. "What's the real reason?"

"My dad was a cop. He took a bullet on the job and died when I was twenty. I didn't have any family, so I dropped out of college and applied to the Boston PD." She shrugged. "Felt like the right thing to do. Cops were the only family I ever knew."

"What about your mom?" Chloe found her curiosity about Dana suddenly insatiable. She'd have to pace herself with the questions.

"I don't remember much about her. She died in a car accident when I was three." Dana removed her snowshoes and set them in the back of the SUV. "What about you? Why'd you want to be a cop?"

"I had my life figured out the moment I saw my very first rerun of *Cagney and Lacey.*"

Dana laughed. "I loved that show!"

She smiled, remembering when her purpose in life became clear. "I was ten. Couldn't wait to hit the streets and bring down the bad guys. I even cut my hair really short to look like Christine Cagney, but then everyone thought I was a boy." She met Dana's gaze and laughed.

Dana's eyes lingered on hers. "I bet you were gorgeous, even back then."

Chloe felt the connection between them sizzle. She swallowed, unable to tear herself from Dana's gaze. Those eyes—so deep, so dark, so *knowing*—could reel her in and make her forget everything else.

"Hungry?" Dana asked.

"Starving."

"I make a mean fettuccini Alfredo."

"I make a mean salad." Chloe admittedly wasn't much of a cook.

They stopped at the store to pick up salad fixings, fresh garlic, gourmet cheeses, and a bottle of wine. Chloe found herself suddenly anxious in line at the register. This was beginning to feel like a date.

CHAPTER TEN

Back at Dana's, they showered, changed, and met in the kitchen. Chloe poured the wine while Dana lit some candles and started dinner. Yo-Yo Ma's Bach Cello Suites sounded over the kitchen speakers.

With the meal prepped and the table set, they sat down for a leisurely dinner. The conversation came naturally, the mood light. Chloe found herself liking this woman more and more.

They cleared the table, loaded the dishwasher, and retreated to the living room. Chloe slid off her shoes and curled her feet underneath her on the sofa, her mind quieted by the conversation, her body warmed by the wine.

"How about a fire?" Dana asked.

"Sounds good." Chloe sipped her wine, a little nervous about Dana's expectations at the end of the night. "Okay…is this a date?" she asked, her stomach suddenly tying in knots.

Long seconds ticked by before Dana responded, "Do you want it to be a date?"

Self-doubt crept in at warp speed. Chloe wasn't sure how to answer. Her mind darted in several directions at once. What was she thinking? There was no way Dana could ever be attracted to her—not after what she just saw in Maribel's office. And certainly not after her meltdown at the condo. Not to mention the fact that Dana was a widow whose wife's killer was still stalking her with hidden cameras. Now that she thought about it, the hand-holding in the car was probably out of pity. She was crazy for letting the idea of a date even enter her mind. "Forget I asked. Can I blame that moment of delirium on the wine?" She took several long sips, wishing she could spontaneously combust right there in Dana's living room, never to be seen or heard from again.

Dana was quiet for so long Chloe became convinced she had ruined the budding friendship between them. Fire started, Dana turned and met Chloe's gaze with a forthright confidence she found amazingly sexy. "I'd like this to be our first date."

Chloe let out the breath she was holding. "You could've said that an hour ago when I asked the question. I've been sitting here wondering if I'd just ruined our chance of being friends."

"I think we both know we're already past friends. And if I'm totally honest, I felt that the moment we met."

"Me, too," Chloe admitted, thinking back to their encounter at the café.

"What I don't want to happen is for you to feel rushed into anything. You're dealing with enough right now. The last thing you need is any pressure. I have zero expectations, Chloe. We can move at whatever pace you want and need." Dana sat beside her on the couch and leaned over to kiss her on the cheek. "I'm not going anywhere."

Chloe felt her eyes well up against her will. She had no idea if she had anything left to give after what Sylvio had taken. "Sorry. Must be the wine," she said, feeling foolish. She stood and retreated to the kitchen to rinse her wineglass and call it a night.

Dana walked up slowly beside her. "Talk to me. What's going on?"

She set her wineglass on the counter and dried her hands on a dish towel. "Part of me is excited by the thought of being with you. But an even bigger part is terrified. What happened changed me, Dana. The way I see myself is different now." She shook her head. "He left scars on my body. How could you possibly be attracted to me after what he did?"

"What he did is not who you are. I'm drawn to you because you're smart, funny, strong, independent, and beautiful—inside and out. You're still all of those things and more, in spite of what he did to you." Dana slid her hands down Chloe's hips and pulled her close.

Suddenly aware of the heat between them, Chloe's breath caught in her throat as their bodies pressed together. Even in jeans and a sweater, Dana was unbelievably sexy.

"If it makes you feel better, I haven't even kissed anyone since Gabbi. I haven't felt ready. It's important to give ourselves the time we need for things to feel okay again."

Chloe thought about that for a moment. Dana might not have been abducted and held against her will like Gabbi, but she needed time to heal just the same.

She studied Dana's lips. A warm natural shade, they were full and slightly moist. She wanted to feel them on hers in the worst way, but she wasn't ready.

Dana seemed to sense her ambivalence. "No expectations. Okay?"

Nodding, she moved into Dana's arms. Their bodies fit well. Dana was just an inch or two taller. It had been so long since she'd allowed anyone to get this close. Surrendering herself to the embrace, she pressed her body against Dana's.

They hugged and danced slowly in the darkened kitchen, the only source of light three flickering tea light candles on the windowsill. After several minutes, Dana kissed her sweetly on the side of her neck. "In time, you'll find your way back to feeling comfortable inside your own body again," she whispered. "We'll go slow." Then, without another word, Dana turned and walked away.

Chloe brought a hand to her neck. Her skin still burned where Dana's lips had been. It had been a long time since she'd felt the touch of a woman. It was very different from a man's—so much softer, sweeter, and seductive. She blew out the candles on the windowsill and headed off to bed.

❖

Dana awoke with a hand on her throat. The muzzle of a gun was quickly shoved inside her mouth. "Move and you die," said a husky voice in her ear. After mentally calculating her chances of reaching the nightstand, she decided it was just too risky to go for her gun.

The hand around her neck felt too small to be Sylvio's. Besides, she knew he was still in custody. He had obviously hired another goon to do his dirty work. She wondered if this was the same guy who shot at them yesterday. How the hell did he bypass her security system?

Her next thought was on Chloe downstairs. Was she okay? In a two-story home, burglars usually assumed the bedrooms were on the second floor. She hoped that was the case with this guy. With any luck, he'd found her first but hadn't found Chloe yet.

Why hadn't Taz alerted them to the intruder in the house? Some guard dog he was. If she made it out of this alive, she had every intention of sitting down and having a little chat with him.

❖

Chloe sat up in bed and looked at the clock: 2:53 a.m. Taz had woken her with a gentle nudge to her hand. "What's up, boy?" He never woke her up in the middle of the night. "Potty trip?" she whispered.

He cocked his head at the door and growled in warning.

She held her breath and listened to the stillness of Dana's house, letting her eyes adjust to the darkness.

Absolute silence. Not even the ticking of a clock or the hum of the refrigerator. When she climbed out of bed, she felt a chill in the air. She knelt down and waved her hands over the baseboard heater. It was cool.

If they'd lost electricity, why were the numbers on the alarm clock still glowing? She followed the cord to the outlet, unplugged it, and almost laughed aloud when the numbers continued to glow. Efficient as ever, Dana had apparently loaded the clock with backup batteries in case the power went out.

A creak on the wooden floor just outside her bedroom door put her entire body on alert. Taz crept over to a space at the foot of the bed, lay down, and remained perfectly still. Watching him, she was reminded of a lion waiting to ambush unsuspecting prey. She slid the nightstand drawer open, withdrew her 9 mm, and watched as the doorknob turned. Out of habit, she'd locked it before climbing into bed.

Moving on pure instinct, she slid two pillows underneath the blankets, arranged them to look like a body, and ducked behind the rocking chair in the corner. She peered between the wooden slats of the chair, listening as the intruder picked the lock on the other side, quietly, effortlessly.

Goose bumps broke out on her arms and legs. She clicked the safety off and watched as the intruder stepped inside. Dressed in black from head to toe, he held his gun out in front of him. At about five eleven, one hundred and sixty pounds, he had a lean build. Too small to be Sylvio. She noticed the gun was fitted with a silencer, and that's when it hit her...What about Dana? Had he already gotten to Dana upstairs? Is that what had alerted Taz? Her mouth went dry, and her stomach somersaulted.

She watched as the man boldly walked over to the bed, pointed his gun at where her head would have been, and pulled the trigger without a moment's hesitation. Poor bastard had no idea what was coming.

Taz was on top of him before he knew it. Trained to recognize a weapon and disarm a suspect, he clamped down on the man's arm and shook his head violently from side to side.

The gun skidded across the floor. Taz released him and stepped back, keeping him cornered against the wall with a show of his teeth. The man withdrew another gun from the small of his back as Chloe was standing. He took aim at Taz. She didn't bother identifying herself as a police officer. She raised her 9 mm. Aimed. Fired.

A perfect shot, center chest. He reeled back, cracked his head against the wall, and slid to the floor. She knelt in the dark and felt for a pulse. Nothing. The bastard hadn't even given her enough credit to wear a bulletproof vest.

"You okay, boy?" she whispered.

Taz whined and licked her face nervously, as if asking her the same.

"I'm fine. Thanks for your help." She kissed his muzzle. "We need to check on Dana."

She stood and tiptoed from the bedroom, wondering if there was a second gunman in the house. If so, he'd probably heard the gunshot. That might turn out to be a good thing if it took the attention off Dana.

Stealthy as ever, Taz led the way. She followed him barefoot down the hall, through the kitchen, and across the living room. Her heartbeat thundered in her ears as she hugged the wall and silently ascended the stairs.

Every muscle in her body was tense and ready to fight. All she could think of was Dana upstairs alone. What would she find when she got there? Chloe fought back the tears and kept moving until she reached Dana's bedroom door. It was open.

She squatted down beside Taz and listened, planning their next move, when she heard Dana's voice saying, "My name is Dana Blake. I'm a detective with the Boston Po—"

"You think I care?"

Even though she knew Sylvio was in custody, Chloe breathed a sigh of relief when she realized the voice wasn't his.

"Maybe not," Dana said, sounding as calm as ever. "But you might care about sitting on death row for murdering a police officer."

"Don't worry. I'm not gonna kill you," he snarled. "But trust me, I ain't doin' you any favors because you'll wish you were dead after tonight."

Chloe inched to the doorway and peered inside. The streetlamp outside illuminated the bedroom enough for her to make out Dana's shape. She was sitting in the armchair near the window, and it looked like she was handcuffed. The perp stood off to one side. He was holding a gun to her head.

The floorboards suddenly betrayed her. She drew in a breath as he shot a glance in her direction, raised his weapon, and fired.

The bullet whizzed dangerously close to Taz. She grabbed hold of his collar and yanked him back as slivers of the doorframe rained down around them. "Police!" she shouted, now hidden from view. "Lower your weapon. We have you surrounded."

"Bullshit!" he yelled back. "No cops here. Just you. You're the bitch from downstairs."

"I'm a police officer," she corrected. "I've already called for backup."

"Like hell you did. We shut off the power."

"Ever hear of a cell phone, asshole?" As long as she kept him talking, he was paying attention to her and not to Dana. Unfortunately, the part about calling in for backup was a lie. She'd been so amped up from the shooting she hadn't even thought to unplug her cell from the charger downstairs and dial 911. She felt like giving herself a big dope slap.

"What the fuck did you do to my partner?"

"Calm down. He's in custody." Technically dead and in custody. But still in custody.

"Show me your face or she dies."

Dana pleaded from the other side, "Don't listen to him."

"Shut up!" he yelled.

She heard scuffling. "I'm fine," Dana said. "Stay there, Chloe."

"You don't listen too good, do you?"

Chloe sensed the situation taking a turn for the worse. She couldn't let Dana die while she sat here and did nothing. She gave Taz a hand signal to stay, set her gun on the floor, and stepped in front of the doorway with her hands up. "Okay. I'm here. Calm down."

Poised to strike Dana with the butt of his gun, he turned and pointed the gun at her. He yanked Dana to her feet and held her in front of him as a shield.

"I'm unarmed," Chloe said. "Let's talk this out, you and me. We know you were sent here by someone else, so it's not you we're interested in."

"Shit," he said, whistling obnoxiously. "I heard you were hot, but now you make me want to sample the goods before I put a bullet in your head."

Chloe's stomach turned. There was no way in hell she'd ever let that happen.

He slid his free hand between the buttons of Dana's silk pajamas and yanked down, popping the buttons off as he went. "You're both sexy as hell. Maybe we could have a little threesome."

Dana caught her eye and mouthed, *On three.* Chloe knew instantly what Dana wanted her to do.

Dana counted on her fingers, one at a time. On three, she lifted her feet from the floor and used her weight to throw him off balance.

Chloe gave Taz the attack command. He came barreling around the corner like a cannon, leaped in the air, and ripped into the perp's arm with a fury she had never seen from him before. The gun went off as Chloe dived to the ground. She grabbed her 9 mm behind the wall, rolled to her back, and shouted at Taz to back off. She wasn't taking any chances this time. The perp could be armed with a backup like his partner downstairs.

She pulled the trigger the second Taz was out of the line of fire. Her bullet landed square in the middle of the bastard's chest. He staggered back and sank to the floor, his mouth slack, his eyes wide with surprise.

Dana bent down to retrieve his gun as Chloe stepped over and felt for a pulse. Two perps in one night was a record for her.

"You were amazing, boy," she said, checking Taz from nose to tail for any signs of injury. Satisfied he was unharmed, she fished the handcuff key out of the dead man's pocket, stood, and met Dana's gaze.

Dana held out her wrists.

She felt a ball of dread in her stomach as she unlocked the cuffs. "Did he—"

"No." Dana closed the front of her shirt and held it shut. "He didn't."

Chloe wanted to stay calm, but her shaking hands gave her away. Knowing she'd almost lost Dana was more than she could handle. She sat on the edge of the bed and stared at the corpse on the floor. "I was afraid I'd find you up here..."

"I'm okay." Dana sat down beside her. "Where's the partner he talked about?"

"Dead." She met Dana's eyes. "I'm so sorry I brought you into this."

"I'm not." Dana stared at her lips.

The air between them sizzled. Again, she found herself wondering what it would be like to kiss Dana. She felt a lightning bolt of anticipation shoot straight to her core.

Dana took a deep breath and sighed. "Maybe we'd both be safer if we started sleeping together at night."

The moment broken, Chloe laughed. She was just grateful the three of them were still in one piece.

Dana knelt in front of Taz, grabbed him by the sides of his face, and kissed his nose loudly. "I'm getting you a superhero cape for Christmas."

Taz wagged his tail proudly and kissed her back.

❖

Dana dialed BPD's backline to report the break-in and request some squad cars. She didn't want this call going out over the radio and potentially tipping their hand to Sylvio that she and Chloe were still alive.

Leaving Chloe on the bed with her 9 mm and Taz for protection, she grabbed a flashlight from the nightstand, went to her walk-in closet, and selected two changes of clothes. Sirens sounded in the distance as she and Chloe shed their pajamas in the dark, side by side.

Stepping into her jeans, Dana knew what happened tonight was way too close for comfort. She caught a glimpse of Chloe's silhouette in the dark and promised herself she would never underestimate Sylvio again.

CHAPTER ELEVEN

Both she and Dana had changed out of their pajamas and into regular clothes by the time the police arrived. She was glad Dana had the wherewithal to think that far ahead. She was already feeling awkward enough without walking around half naked in front of a bunch of cops. They gave their statements, turned the bodies over to the ME, and put a call in to Maribel.

"My alarm doesn't go off for another hour. This better be good."

Chloe watched the ME zip up the first body bag. "Looks like there's a price on our heads."

"Speak for yourself," Dana called out from across the room. "They wanted me alive."

"Are you okay?" Maribel asked, suddenly sounding bright-eyed and bushy-tailed.

"I stand corrected," Chloe said. "From the looks of my pillow, they definitely wanted *me* dead. But we think they had plans to take Dana with them." The police had already found a duffel bag with chloroform, handcuffs, and duct tape. They hadn't located the getaway car yet, but it was only a matter of time. They'd probably find it later when one of the neighbors woke up and reported a suspicious vehicle parked where it didn't belong. Or maybe there was a third partner—a driver—who'd wisely fled the scene as soon as he heard sirens approaching.

Whatever the case, it was obviously a well-organized operation. Not only had the men managed to bypass Dana's security system, but they'd actually had the balls to mess with two cops. The next step in the investigation would be to trace the two dead men back to Sylvio, but that could be tricky. More than likely, Sylvio had gone to great lengths to cover his tracks.

Chloe filled Maribel in on the night's events but left out the part about Dana being groped. Too many cop ears in the room. And cops liked to talk.

Maribel sighed into the phone. "We need to get the two of you to a safe house. I'll make the arrangements. Call you back in a few."

They hung up. Chloe stared at the phone. Did Maribel say *safe house*? She had no intention of being locked away in a safe house when she and Dana could be helping with this case.

Dana came up beside her. "What's going on?"

Chloe brought her hand to her shoulder and started rubbing the knot there. "Maribel said something about finding us a safe house."

"Where?"

"I don't know. She'll call us back soon with the details."

"So what's the problem?"

Chloe shook her head. "Tonight was too close. I couldn't handle it if Sylvio got to you."

"Sylvio's in jail. We can handle the goons he sends."

She crossed her arms, all too aware of how close Dana was standing. "Maybe it would be best if we parted ways here—"

"I am *not* tucking tail and stepping aside just because things got a little hairy. Where you go, I go. That's been the deal from the beginning, and it's not going to change until we see this through to the end. What you decide to do with your life after that is entirely up to you. But you're stuck with me until he's behind bars for good and I know you're safe."

Chloe's cell rang. Maribel.

"Pack your bags and meet me at the station in thirty minutes. Have one of the officers there drive you. I'll fill you in on the rest later. Put Dana on."

She passed the phone to Dana, halfway hoping Maribel would tell her she was no longer needed and free to return to her usual job.

Dana listened for a moment, her eyes on Chloe. "Both were clean shots to the chest. She seems to be doing just fine." A short pause with more listening. "Okay. See you in thirty." She ended the call and glanced at her watch. "Better hurry and pack what we can. I'm not sure how long we'll be gone."

Chloe nodded and headed off to the guest room, feeling more and more unsettled with every passing minute. It was clear to her now that Dana was Sylvio's next target. There was one thing she knew for sure about Sylvio: he wouldn't give up until he got exactly what he wanted.

❖

Dana threw some clothes in a duffel bag and packed some toiletries. How could Chloe have even suggested they part ways? Did Chloe really think she would agree to that? Granted, they were still getting to know one another, but...come on. When it came to not quitting, Dana was an expert. She didn't know how to give up. It just wasn't in her DNA.

She shook her head, realizing Chloe was only trying to keep her safe. They were two cops doing what they were trained to do—trying to protect each other. This is exactly why she didn't date cops. For this very reason right here.

Chloe had already been through enough. It was up to Dana to be vigilant and keep her eye on the ball from now on. Her job was to keep Chloe safe, and she was committed to that plan at all costs. Chloe's job was to focus on recovering her memories of what happened. She couldn't do that if she was constantly looking over her shoulder for danger. It was that simple.

Determined to step up her game, Dana zipped her duffel bag and headed downstairs to check on Chloe. A safe house was a good idea. The best course of action right now was to drop off Sylvio's radar until the trial.

❖

"Wardsboro?" Chloe said, rolling her eyes.

Maribel looked exhausted. In jeans and a red wool sweater, she leaned back in the captain's chair and brought her fingers to her temples. "Don't argue with me, Chloe. I had to call in a lot of favors for this. The cabin is owned by a recently retired judge. He's agreed to give up a season of skiing so the two of you can be safe."

A *season* of skiing? Her stomach bottomed out. "My God. How long will we be there?"

"The trial is set for May sixth—"

"But we're only halfway through November!"

"You'll be there through the duration of the trial. I'm sorry, there's just no wiggle room on this."

"Great." Feeling a headache coming on, she pinched the bridge of her nose. "What are we supposed to do? Just leave our jobs here at the department and then pop back in six months from now to pick up where we left off?"

"That's exactly what you're going to do." Maribel cast a glance at Dana. "To anyone who asks, you're both working a case. You'll be returning to your normal duties as soon as this assignment is over. The only one who knows the real story is your captain."

Chloe turned to Dana. "What about your active cases?"

"Some of them can wait," Dana replied. "The ones that can't will be shuffled out to the other detectives."

"What about the victims? The ones you've already built a rapport with. They trust you, Dana."

"The only victim who matters to me right now is you—"

"I am *not* a victim." She clenched her jaw.

"You were two years ago." Dana met her gaze, unapologetic. "You may have been a Tisbury cop back then, but you're part of our family now. We protect our own. It's that simple." She rose from her chair, turned, and walked out, shutting the door firmly behind her.

Chloe and Maribel sat in silence.

"I've known Dana a long time," Maribel said finally. "You can trust her. If you're not ready, she won't push you."

Chloe looked up, confused. "Not ready for what?"

"It's clear the two of you have a connection. What I see between you two reminds me of what was there between her and Gabbi."

Chloe felt the heat intensify in her cheeks as she squirmed in the resultant quiet.

"Gabbi and I went back a long time," Maribel went on, seemingly happy to fill the silence. "Best friends since seventh grade. I knew everything about her, and she knew me better than anyone. Gabbi couldn't stop talking about Dana after they met. They went out to lunch at the same restaurant where I happened to be meeting a friend. When Gabbi introduced me, I knew instantly."

"Knew what?" Chloe asked, curiosity getting the best of her.

"I knew they were meant for each other. But Gabbi still didn't have a clue, so I kept quiet and waited until she figured it out."

"Did she ever talk to you about it?"

"Eventually. It was hard for her, though. She'd never been attracted to a woman. She'd never even entertained the possibility she was anything but straight. What I do know is she and Dana ended up really happy together." She studied Chloe. "Are you scared to be alone with Dana?"

"Not in the way you're thinking." Chloe frowned. "I'm scared something will happen to her if she stays with me. I can't handle Dana getting hurt—not after what happened to Michael."

Maribel walked around the desk to sit in the chair beside her. "I can work it out with your captain and send someone else to go with you to Vermont if that's what you want. It's up to you."

Chloe was momentarily conflicted. Part of her wanted nothing more than time alone with Dana in a cozy cabin up north. Another part insisted it would be a mistake that could very well end up costing Dana her life. She knew she could never live with herself if that happened.

She took a deep breath and met Maribel's gaze. "Get someone else."

There. She'd said it. Her decision was made. If Sylvio was taking her down, she'd go down alone.

Dana was cleaning her gun when Maribel sat in the chair beside her desk. When she didn't say anything, Dana glanced up. She knew that expression all too well. Bad news was in the air. She set her gun aside. "What's up?"

"Captain Hernandez will be calling you into his office soon. I just wanted to give you a heads-up. He's assigning Hunter to the protective detail."

"I don't need Hunter. I can handle this on my own." Hunter would only get in the way.

"That's not what Chloe wants."

"She asked for two cops?" Dana found that hard to believe.

Maribel shook her head slowly. "She asked for one."

Chloe was cleaning out her locker when she heard Dana storm in behind her.

Dana was fuming. "What the hell do you think you're doing?"

"Sanitizing." She held up the Lysol wipes in her hand.

"Captain said he's sending Hunter in my place."

She caught a whiff of Dana's perfume. God, what was it about this woman she found so alluring? "Did he say why?"

"No. But my savvy detective instincts are telling me you asked for the switch." Dana stung her with sad eyes.

She slung her duffel bag over one shoulder and stood. "I'd never forgive myself if something happened to you. Just try and under—"

"Nothing you say right now could make me understand why you did this," Dana said. "What you're doing is selfish, irresponsible, and just plain stupid."

Chloe scanned the locker room. Deserted. She set her duffel bag down on the bench and stepped forward to give Dana a long hug. "Thank you."

"For what?" Dana asked.

Chloe brushed her lips against Dana's ear. "For caring." She drew back and peered into Dana's eyes. "I don't want to lose this."

"And I don't want you to put your life in the hands of an out-of-shape cop who probably couldn't do a lap around the track without a dogsled team."

Chloe could hardly believe what she was about to do. She brushed her lips against Dana's and gently probed along their edges, using just the tip of her tongue. Dana's lips were exquisitely soft. Finished with testing the waters, Chloe decided she wanted more.

Dana seemed to sense her decision. She backed Chloe up against the locker, and their eyes locked, the desire clear in Dana's. "Are you sure?" she whispered.

Her chest heaving, she nodded.

It was Dana who made the first move this time. She brought her lips to Chloe's and kissed her so softly, so sweetly, that it made her want to cry.

Chloe opened her mouth, inviting her inside. Dana tasted like cinnamon chewing gum. Their tongues danced in unison, each of them hungry for more. At that moment, she knew what they'd be like in bed together. Dana would take her time getting to know her body. She'd touch Chloe slowly, helping to reacquaint her with what it felt like to make love. They'd take turns pleasing each other in ways Chloe could only begin to imagine. And through it all, she'd feel so connected to Dana, so intimately a part of her.

Dana still had her pinned up against the locker. The contrast between Dana's firm grip on her arms and the softness of her lips and tongue was strangely erotic.

By the time Dana pulled away, they were both out of breath.

Maribel cleared her throat behind them. "Sorry to interrupt."

Dana released her and turned in surprise. "How long have you been standing there?"

"Long enough to know the two of you look really good together." She winked at Chloe. "Hunter's waiting for you outside."

"Hold on," Dana said, tucking a blond curl behind Chloe's ear. "Can I have that?" She pointed to a strawberry-flavored ChapStick on the locker shelf.

"I've already used it. But there's a whole box of them in my bottom desk drawer that are unopened—"

"I want that one."

Grinning, she reached up and handed Dana the ChapStick.

❖

"There must be some mistake," Dana said.

Maribel handed her the leash. "No mistake."

Dana stared at the leash in disbelief. Chloe would never leave without Taz.

"He's still in the patrol car outside," Maribel explained. "She gave me explicit instructions no one other than you is to open that car. Said something about someone not having a face." She tossed Dana the keys, hugged her, and turned to leave. "It'll be okay, Dana. Just take care of Taz until she comes back."

But Dana feared Chloe was never coming back. Chloe was obviously thinking the same. She thought back to Sylvio's red German shepherd tie at the arraignment. That clever but subtle threat to Taz wasn't lost on Chloe. She was leaving Taz behind with Dana to keep him out of harm's way.

"Dammit," Dana said aloud, tears blurring her vision. Chloe was leaving them both behind to keep them safe…because she didn't believe she was going to make it out of this alive.

Dana pulled herself together and made her way to the department parking lot. She laughed out loud when she saw the notes taped to each of the windows: *Do Not Open Unless You Know a Good Plastic Surgeon.* Chloe had managed somehow to keep her sense of humor in all of this. That, above all else, showed Dana just how strong she was.

She held down the button on the keychain to unlock the rear doors. Taz's head popped up immediately from the back seat. He recognized her before she even got to the car, made clear by his wagging tail and wriggling body.

She opened the rear door but blocked his path of escape. "Listen up, bud," she said, holding his large head between her hands. "Chloe had to leave for a little while, so you and I will be spending some time together. There are some ground rules we need to go over."

Taz sat in the back seat, cocked his head, and peered into her eyes.

"No outwardly aggressive behavior toward any of my brothers and sisters in blue. That means no growling, no teeth baring, no barking, and definitely no biting. Got it?"

He didn't take his eyes from hers.

She was about to go on when Fred approached from behind. "Hey, Dana. Who are you talking to?"

"Behave," she whispered. She gave Taz the evil eye and stepped back.

"Is that the dog who kicked ass this morning and saved two cops?"

"One of those cops was me," Dana said, clipping the leash to Taz's collar. "And yes, he saved my life." She stepped aside to let him jump down from the car.

"Hell of a dog you got there. We've met before. Everyone's calling him a hero." Fred reached into the cargo pocket of his uniform and handed Taz a tiny dog biscuit in the shape of a bone. "Shame they kicked him out of K-9 school," he said, frowning.

"You heard about that?" She watched as Taz accepted the biscuit and gently nudged Fred's hand for more.

Fred obliged, emptying both pockets a biscuit at a time. "His handler's a dickwad. Wouldn't know a good dog if it bit him in the ass." He slapped Taz affectionately on the shoulder. "I'd take you as my partner any day, champ."

Dana frowned. If she didn't know any better, she'd swear this dog was smiling. She looked up at Fred. "Can you give us a lift? I left my car at home this morning."

"Sure thing. Patrol car's out front."

"We'll meet you there. Give me a minute inside first."

She turned to Taz as Fred walked out of earshot. "How about you and me blow this joint and go find Chloe?"

He wagged his tail at the mention of Chloe's name.

Proud to be by his side, she led Taz into the station. She'd be damned if she was going to let Chloe face this alone. And if Taz could talk, she was pretty sure he'd have already blasted her for not thinking of it sooner.

But first things first. Like every other Boston cop, Taz needed to be fitted with a bulletproof vest.

CHAPTER TWELVE

H ope you don't mind Christmas a little early," Hunter said from the driver's seat. He unzipped a black leather case and pulled out a Bing Crosby Christmas CD.

"Not at all." Chloe smiled. "Who doesn't love Bing?"

He popped the CD in the car stereo, turned up the volume, and drove out of the station parking lot.

Hunter was a solid cop with a good reputation. She'd heard through the grapevine that Hunter and his partner, Hopkins, had worked the streets together for ten years. They even tested for detective at the same time and transferred as a pair. Second day on the job, some teenage kid high on meth held up a convenience store. Hopkins walked in to buy some lottery tickets and was dead five minutes later, shot three times at close range. Apparently, Hunter had never been the same after that.

Chloe felt a kinship with him. She understood what it was like to have someone important taken from you unexpectedly. Felt like your soul was being ripped out by the roots.

He wasn't much of a talker, but she was grateful for the quiet. It would give her time to think...about the case...the upcoming trial...Dana.

Had she made a mistake leaving Dana behind? Instincts told her she'd made the right choice. If Sylvio's goons managed to track her to Vermont, things would get ugly. Well, uglier. She knew more about how Sylvio's mind worked than she cared to admit. If he made bail and found Dana and Chloe at the cabin together, he'd make Dana his next victim. There was no doubt in her mind about that. She shuddered at the thought. It was best for everyone—and safer for Dana—if someone who hadn't already captured Sylvio's eye took over her protective detail.

She missed Taz already and hoped he and Dana would get along okay without her. Maybe they'd be good for each other. She'd left Taz behind for his own safety, but it also made her feel better knowing Dana had some extra protection. He'd protect Dana with his life, if it came down to that.

She glanced at Hunter as he sang along to "Silent Night." He actually had a pretty good voice. "How long until we get there?" she asked.

"About five hours."

She stared out the window as they merged onto I-95. Her eyelids grew heavy. She'd only slept an hour or two the night before. No wonder she was so tired. She'd been running on pure adrenaline since the shootings.

She tilted her seat back, pulled her coat around herself, and closed her eyes. Images of the two dead gunmen flashed through her mind. Chloe was relieved—though slightly disturbed—to discover she didn't feel a shred of guilt over their deaths. The steady thrum of the engine and warm air from the vents soon lulled her into sleepy remembrances of Dana's lips on hers.

❖

"Son of a bitch!"

Chloe's eyes popped open at the sound of Hunter's voice.

"Get down!" he shouted from the driver's seat. "They're behind us." He held out his arm and covered her protectively, his left hand still on the wheel.

She heard shots fired, too many in a row to count. Whoever was following them had an automatic weapon. One of the bullets must have pierced the rear tire because the car suddenly swerved out of control. "Hang on!" Cursing under his breath, Hunter fought with the steering wheel.

Everything was happening so fast. Chloe tried to shake off the sleepy stupor still buzzing inside her head. She reached for the gun at her hip as their car jerked wildly back and forth on the road. She watched the speedometer needle dip from 70 to 60...45...40. Hunter grabbed his weapon as the car scraped against the guardrail, the sound of metal against metal screeching in her ears.

Their car came to rest on the opposite side of the road. They were both hunched over on the seat, practically nose to nose. "Where are we?" she whispered, kicking herself for falling asleep.

"Haven't a goddamn clue. Hit a detour a while back," he whispered, his breath ripe with chocolate. "Kept following the signs, but I haven't seen a car in a while."

Typical. A man who couldn't stop and ask for directions. Great. And now they had no idea where the hell they were. An empty king-sized M&M's bag crinkled under her elbow. "I can't believe you didn't offer me any," she said, holding up the wrapper.

"What'd you want me to do?" Hunter asked. "Wake you up just to offer you some?"

Rapid gunfire suddenly broke out around them. They ducked down and huddled closer until a deathly silence commenced.

"That would've been the considerate thing to do, Hunter."

"Well, shit. I'm sorry."

She cautiously peered over the seat. "Black SUV about fifty yards away. Tinted windows. No movement." She ducked back down as another spray of bullets pierced the car's exterior.

"One of those rounds is gonna hit our gas tank." He reached over and cut the engine. "Want to stay in here and wait for the Fourth of July?"

"Not particularly." Since Hunter was older and no doubt slower than she was, he'd make an easy target. She didn't like where this was going.

Before either of them could make a move, she heard car doors opening and men's voices, followed by another spray of bullets as the men drew closer. This time, one of the rounds grazed Hunter's receding hairline. Blood trickled down the front of his face.

He brought his hand to his face and wiped at the blood. "Play dead," he whispered, reaching over to smear his blood across the front of her sweater. He sat up, his 9 mm tucked between his thighs. She had no idea what he had planned and didn't have time to ask. The men were almost upon them now, approaching the car from both sides. She glanced in the side view mirror. Looked like there were only two of them.

Exaggerating his own injury, he started gasping for breath. "Bastards!" he croaked. "You killed her!"

She squinted her eyes open just enough to see the man outside Hunter's window lift his rifle, obviously intent on spraying the interior of the car. Hunter paid no attention to the man on his side. He was focused on protecting her from the man on hers.

Hunter slid his gun out from between his thighs and fired, spiderwebbing the passenger's window around the bullet hole.

She raised her own gun a millisecond later, but her semi-automatic pistol couldn't compete with an automatic at the ready. Hunter's body jerked with the impact of each bullet. She squeezed the trigger and shot the gunman point-blank in the center of his chest. Unlike his comrades earlier at Dana's, this guy was wearing a vest.

Her second bullet landed in the middle of his face and blew out the back of his skull.

She leaned over Hunter and peered out the window to make sure the gunman was dead. Definitely dead. Dead and pretty much faceless.

Three in one day. She was on a roll.

She holstered her weapon and eased back from Hunter. His clothes were soaked in blood, his body riddled with holes. So many holes. "Oh God." Tears spilled down her cheeks as she wiped the blood from his eyes. "I'm so sorry."

"Don't be." He waved a bloody hand as he gasped for air. "Truth is…I miss my old partner too damn much. Ain't nothing to look forward to anymore." His throat made a gurgling sound as blood bubbled from one corner of his mouth.

She smoothed his graying hair and held his hand. "I'm right here with you, Hunter."

Struggling to draw another breath, he gave her hand a gentle squeeze.

"I never got a chance to meet Hopkins," she said. "Make sure you tell him you're my hero."

Hunter smiled proudly as his eyes focused on something far, far away.

She sat beside his body for long minutes. Blood coated her hands, jeans, and gray sweater. Hunter's blood.

Memories of her final moments with Sylvio returned with a vengeance. His deep, gritty voice resounded in her mind: *Nothing like the smell of blood from a dead cop.* He'd said those words over and over as he'd beat her to within an inch of her life.

She opened the car door and threw up on the pavement. The dead gunman stared blankly at the sky just a few feet away. This wasn't supposed to happen. None of this was supposed to happen. Silence lapped at the edges of her sanity until she was half convinced she was the only living thing left on the planet.

Dana clicked on her Bluetooth and answered. "Detective Blake."

"Where are you?" Maribel asked.

"In the car." She reached over to give Taz a pat on the back. After having saved her life, the very least she could do was extend him the courtesy of riding in the front seat.

"Hunter was supposed to check in thirty minutes ago. I haven't heard from him. When I call, it goes straight to voicemail."

Alarm bells went off inside Dana's head. She white-knuckled the steering wheel.

"I'm here at the station," Maribel went on. "Stephens tracked Chloe's cell by IMEI, but it's no longer in transit. Looks like they stopped somewhere near Wardsboro."

Dana glanced at her GPS. "I'm about twenty minutes from Wardsboro now."

"You are?" Maribel asked, sounding momentarily surprised. "Of course you are. Where else would you be? Is Taz there with you?"

"Affirmative. He wanted in on the action."

"I already called the Vermont State Police. They're on their way. Be careful, Dana. As the best friend who readily filled the shoes of my deceased best friend, you have an obligation to stay alive."

Dana was honored. They'd never spoken of their friendship status aloud, but the feeling was mutual. "Roger that," she said. "And ditto."

❖

Chloe jogged along the road, trying to get a service bar to appear on her cell. She was in a dead zone. No pun intended, she thought bitterly. She finally gave up, tucked the phone in her pocket, and trekked back to the gunmen's SUV.

She opened the driver's door and scanned the all-black interior. The front and back seats were immaculate. It smelled brand new. Out of habit, she glanced at the odometer, but it was digital and would only be visible if the keys were in the ignition.

Damn, no keys. Which meant she had the privilege of fishing around in some dead guy's pockets to find them.

She popped the rear door and stepped around to the back. No gear—not even a gum wrapper—had been left behind. Slamming the rear door, she walked back to the dead man on Hunter's side—the bastard she'd shot and killed. Blood, pieces of white skull, and gray brain matter were strewn across the pavement. But it didn't faze her. She'd seen worse on the job as a medic.

She knelt beside him and searched his pockets until her fingers closed around the car remote. She accidentally pushed a button as she withdrew her hand, and the SUV exploded behind her.

The sound was deafening. Pieces of metal flew through the air and skidded across the pavement. She raised her arms protectively in front of her face and took cover near the front bumper of Hunter's car as flames erupted from the SUV's engine.

Chloe looked down at the remote in her hand. The SUV must have been rigged with an explosive—booby-trapped to go off if someone other than the intended driver tried to use it. Sylvio wasn't taking any chances. He'd obviously entertained the possibility she would survive the hit and try to make her way back to civilization in the SUV.

I bet the bastard even set up those detour signs Hunter mentioned. If that was the case, how was help going to find her way out here? She kicked herself now for falling asleep because she had absolutely no idea where she was.

She checked her watch. Ten minutes had passed since they'd crashed and not a single car had come along. Her heart raced as she realized the next car to pull up would probably be Sylvio's reinforcements—sent to clean up the mess and make sure the bodies were never found.

She couldn't risk them arriving and realizing she'd survived. They'd hunt her down for sure and finish the job. She looked around. She was at the base of a mountain. There was nothing but forest and desolate road.

Nowhere to run.

Her breath plumed in front of her as she set to work on the crime scene. She opened the passenger's side door, then dragged the closest of the two gunmen across the pavement, toward the car. His body was still warm. A gust of wind freed some of her curls from the elastic band at her neck. Loose strands tickled her face. She caught a whiff of cologne and gagged. The gunman was wearing L'Eau Bleue. Sylvio's favorite.

Ignoring his stench, she propped him up in the passenger's seat where she had ridden beside Hunter and slammed the door. She grabbed some food and clothes from the back seat and stuffed them inside her backpack as the first few snowflakes fell. She looked up. Clouds had pig-piled, blocking out the sun completely. It was getting late. Maybe an hour of daylight remained.

She went around to the other side, plucked the bloodstained map off the front seat, and folded it with Hunter's blood still inside. She started the engine and unpinned Hunter's badge from the front of his shirt, determined to honor him by keeping it close. She'd give it to a family member later…if she survived.

She opened the gas tank door and unscrewed the cap, then jogged to a safe distance. With a parting prayer for Hunter on her lips, she withdrew her gun, aimed, and fired.

Even though she was prepared this time, the impact of the explosion was titanic. Flames lapped hungrily at the car's interior. It wouldn't take long for the bodies inside to be consumed by fire. By the time rescue arrived, they'd need dental records to identify them.

Sylvio's reinforcements would probably beat the rescue team, which is exactly what Chloe was hoping for. She wanted them to see the remains of two bodies inside the car. With a little luck, they'd assume one of the bodies was hers.

She sprinted along the road for about a mile before veering off into the woods. Her boots sank into virgin powder from a recent storm. Today's snowflakes were falling much too slowly to cover her tracks. She couldn't risk leading them into the woods with her footprints.

She broke off a branch from a nearby pine and swept the furry needles over her tracks as she went. About a hundred yards in, she stopped to inspect her handiwork. If someone wasn't looking for it, her path would be difficult to spot.

She and Hunter were supposed to check in as soon as they reached the cabin. Six hours had passed since they'd left the station. Maribel would start to worry if she didn't hear from them soon. Hopefully, she would send out a search party before Sylvio's reinforcements figured out she was still alive.

A single realization swam up from the depths of her subconscious like a giant dark leviathan. *If Sylvio's men planted those detour signs, they'll probably take them down before a search party convenes.* She prayed someone from the department was tracking her cell.

Deep in the woods now, Chloe tossed the branch aside and plodded forth in the snow. She checked her cell. Still no service. Her best bet was to keep hiking and hope a signal would open up somewhere along her route.

CHAPTER THIRTEEN

Chloe approached the peak, sweating and out of breath. She glanced over her shoulder. Still no sign of Sylvio's men. Her plan to evade capture wouldn't do her much good if she ended up freezing to death overnight on this mountain. She didn't have a book of matches, and the wood on the ground was too wet to start a fire the old-fashioned way.

Darkness was fully upon her now. Last chance, she thought, sliding her phone from her pocket for the hundredth time in the last forty-five minutes. She was staring at the screen when one bar appeared. She wasted no time in dialing Dana's cell.

Dana picked up on the first ring. "Are you okay?"

"I'm on top of a mountain somewhere in the backcountry of Vermont, but I'm fine. I fell asleep in the car." She paused to take a breath. "Hunter said there was a detour. I don't know which exit we got off."

"Keep your phone on. We've been tracking the IMEI. Are you safe?" Dana asked.

"As far as I can tell, nobody followed me here." She heard the hum of an engine on the other end of the line. "Where are you?"

"Almost to Wardsboro. Maribel figured something was wrong when you missed the check-in."

"Turn back," Chloe said. "Hunter's dead." Her eyes welled up with fresh tears. "They shot him, Dana. He died protecting me." She slipped her hand inside her coat pocket and ran her fingers over the cold metal of Hunter's badge.

"I'm sorry. Hunter was a good cop." Dana sighed. "But I'm not turning back. Maribel's been on the phone with the Vermont staties. They found the cars and the bodies inside. I'm just glad one of them isn't yours."

Unsuccessful at convincing Dana to go home, Chloe agreed to stay put until search and rescue arrived. She ended the call, dug a hole in the snow beneath a canopy of pine, and hunkered down to wait in the darkness.

❖

Dana braked to a stop and held her badge out the window to the officers at the scene. "Where's search and rescue?"

The officer pointed to a man and his dog a short distance away. Dana pulled up alongside them and introduced herself.

"Kyle." He withdrew his hand from a neon orange glove and returned the handshake. "This is Oliver." He pointed to the yellow Labrador at his side.

"She said she went up the mountain about a mile down the road. I know what to look for. Follow me." She watched in the rearview mirror as the duo climbed inside their vehicle and pulled up behind her. Resetting the mileage tracker, she drove slowly.

It was dark and difficult to see. Chloe said she'd gone into the woods about a mile from the crime scene, but Dana figured it was an approximate distance and didn't want to miss her point of entry. She withdrew her spotlight from the glove compartment, rolled down the passenger's window, and shined it over the top of the snow. Taz sniffed vigorously at the air as she drove.

She stopped. There were no discernible tracks, but the snow had been disturbed recently. She looked down at the distance traveled and laughed. Exactly one mile.

Taz let out a high-pitched bark. He looked back and forth excitedly from her to the woods.

"You're right," she said, impressed by his superhuman senses as she climbed down from the SUV. "This is where she went up." Taz hopped out after her before she could close the door. He obediently stayed by her side.

"We'll take it from here," Kyle called out as he and Oliver approached.

Dana realized she wasn't suited properly for a hike through the snow. "You'll want to take Taz."

"Is he a certified tracker?"

"Police K-9," she said, happy to bestow the honorable title for the benefit of Taz's astute and very large ears.

"All set. Oliver here is an excellent tracker."

"But Taz knows Chloe." Taz began growling and baring his teeth at Oliver. "This is her dog."

The yellow Lab hid behind Kyle and peeked out from behind his leg.

"Oliver and I work best alone," Kyle said, taking a step back himself. "Your dog has an attitude problem." He adjusted the backpack on his shoulders, turned, and began trekking through the snow alongside Chloe's trail.

Kyle's good looks and enlarged ego got under her skin. "I'll show him what an attitude problem looks like," she said, kneeling beside Taz. His eyes were like laser beams as he watched Kyle and Oliver disappear into the woods. Dana could tell he wanted to follow. His body was tense and quivering with adrenaline.

"I bet you could get to Chloe a lot faster."

Taz cocked his head and directed his gaze to meet hers.

She sighed. "If I let you do this, you cannot bite, maim, or otherwise injure Kyle and Oliver. Got it?"

He barked once, prancing in place.

Dana couldn't believe she was actually talking to this dog like he was a person. In spite of her propensity for rational thinking, she felt certain he understood most of what she said. "When you get to the top, wait with Chloe until Kyle and Oliver get there. Then you can all come back down together." She paused, wondering if there was anything else she should add. "And do *not* get lost. I don't think Kyle and Oliver will want to find you."

Still prancing, he kept his eyes on her face as he awaited her command.

"Okay," she said, hoping she wouldn't regret this later. "Go find Chloe."

Taz took off and headed straight up the mountain like a racehorse.

❖

Chloe was shivering in the hole she'd carved out for herself on the ground. She caught a glimpse of something large as it sprinted toward her in the dark. Were there wolves in Vermont?

She flexed cold fingers, withdrew her 9 mm, and clicked the safety off. Whatever it was, it was coming at her fast. She took a breath and prayed it was traveling alone. She didn't have enough bullets for an entire pack of wolves.

Poised to shoot, she watched as it halted abruptly ten yards away, sniffed the air, and barked.

"Taz?" She lowered her weapon and hugged him as he ran into her arms. His warm body felt so good against hers.

Twenty minutes later, she saw a flashlight bobbing between the trees in the distance. Sweeping the air with big wags of his tail, a yellow Labrador greeted her from about ten feet away. Taz wouldn't let him get any closer.

"Good boy, Oliver!" The orange-suited handler bent down and clipped the leash to Oliver's collar. "Dr. Maddox?"

She nodded and stood as he slipped Oliver a biscuit.

"My name's Kyle. I'm a medic with search and rescue." Striking blue eyes sized her up. "Are you injured?"

Kyle looked like he'd just stepped out of a Brawny paper towel commercial. Six feet, dirty blond hair, ruggedly handsome. "I'm fine. Just cold," she said, flexing stiff fingers.

He peeled off his gloves and cautiously handed them to her, keeping an eye on Taz the whole time. "Here," he said, smiling.

There it was—that look men got when they found her attractive. She glanced at his hand as it brushed against hers. No wedding ring. Butterflies took flight in her stomach as she clumsily pulled at the cuff of one glove to no avail. Her fingers were frozen.

He set Oliver's leash down and stepped forward. "Here, let me."

Her eyes went to the SAR patch on the shoulder of his orange reflective jacket as he fitted the gloves over each of her hands. Even though he was there to help, she didn't like the idea of being alone in the woods with a man she knew nothing about. As if reading her mind, Taz reared up on hind legs, set two paws on Kyle's chest, and growled in warning.

Kyle leaped back in surprise.

"Sorry," she said. "He's a little protective. This is Taz, self-designated bodyguard."

Kyle pressed a button on the radio that was clipped to the shoulder of his jacket. "Missing person located." Frowning, he added, "Four-legged bodyguard also found."

"Ten-four," came a crackly voice from the other end. "Status?"

"Alive and well. No injuries," he reported back.

He handed her a flashlight. They trekked down the mountainside, single file, with Oliver leading the way. Taz had positioned himself between Chloe and Kyle.

They traded medic stories the whole way down, sharing some of their funniest and craziest moments. By the time they reached the bottom, Chloe felt at ease with Kyle and grateful for the banter between them.

Dana climbed out from her SUV and jogged over, hand at the gun on her hip.

Upon seeing Dana, Kyle turned to Chloe. He reached inside his pocket, withdrew a business card, and handed it to her. "I'd love to take you out for dinner sometime."

Eyes the color of tropical waters searched her face. For some reason, Chloe found it hard to look away.

"Think about it." He lifted his backpack from the ground, slung it over one shoulder, and headed toward his vehicle with Oliver in tow.

Chloe glanced down at the card in her hand as Dana stood beside her.

An awkward silence fell between them. "You shouldn't be here," she said, finally meeting Dana's gaze. "You shouldn't be anywhere near me."

Dana's dark eyes clouded with hurt—a vulnerability that was quickly replaced by the gaze she wore as a cop. "I don't trust anyone else to keep you alive," Dana said. "I'm taking you to another safe house."

Chloe unzipped her coat and held it open, revealing her sweater. "If you'd been with me, this would be your blood right now."

"No, it wouldn't. I never would've gotten you into this mess. Hunter was solid, but he made a mistake. The detour signs should have been a red flag. If you were with me, I would've made the calls to find out if the detour was legit."

Chloe said nothing. She knew Dana was right. But she still didn't like the idea that Dana and Taz had come at all. As long as they were with her, their lives were in danger. "Where's the safe house this time?" she asked.

"I'll fill you in later. We need to leave." She grabbed Chloe's backpack from the ground and headed to the SUV.

Chloe walked over to where Kyle stood and handed him his gloves. "Thanks for letting me borrow these."

"Keep them," he said.

"That's okay. I have some." She glanced over at Dana near the SUV. Dana's body language was unmistakable, stiff and uncomfortable as she watched them from afar.

Kyle extended his hand. "It was nice meeting you, Chloe. Oliver and I hope to hear from you soon."

She tucked the business card in his palm as they shook hands. "I'm flattered, but I can't take this."

"Why not?"

She hesitated. "Because I'm already seeing someone."

"Well, keep it," he said. "And if things change—"

"They won't." She took a step forward to give Kyle a hug. It was the first hug she'd allowed from a man in two years. Somehow, with that simple gesture, Chloe managed to reclaim a small part of herself.

She smiled as she walked to Dana's car with Taz at her side. It looked like Sylvio hadn't taken everything from her, after all.

❖

Dana watched as Chloe hugged Kyle. Forcing herself to look away, she couldn't help but wonder if Chloe was attracted to him. There was an obvious chemistry between them. No denying that. A part of her was hurt by this realization. Another deeper part felt proud of Chloe for taking her guard down with a man long enough to hug him. She knew that took a type of resilience and courage most people didn't have.

Whatever was or was not happening between them was none of her business. When it came down to it, Chloe owed her nothing. She was free to hug and date whomever she pleased. Dana's job was still the same: keep Chloe safe. Nothing would change her conviction to see that through.

In that moment, she realized she cared enough about Chloe to support her in whatever way she needed. As a colleague, friend, or as a partner somewhere down the road. She was in Chloe's corner for life.

❖

Exhausted, Chloe kicked off her boots and sank to the bed while Dana checked the closets and bathroom. It was eight thirty a.m. They'd driven all night, changing cars half a dozen times before settling down at a bed-and-breakfast in Ogunquit, Maine. The owner was a trusted friend of Maribel's and had ushered them in from the cold without question.

With Taz at her heels, Dana wedged a chair against the door that led to the hallway.

"There's no way anyone followed us here." Chloe sighed and stared at the ceiling. "Hell, I can't even remember where we are."

"Don't get too comfortable because we're moving to another location tomorrow." Dana sat at a table near the end of the bed. She emptied, cleaned, and reloaded her gun as Taz looked on.

They still had no idea how Sylvio's men had found her. There were only three people who knew about the cabin in Vermont: Maribel, Dana, and Captain Hernandez. Chloe felt confident none of them would have betrayed her. She propped herself up on one elbow. "Can we shop around and sightsee before we go? I haven't been to Maine since I was a kid."

Dana looked over at her like she'd completely lost her mind.

"So...that's a maybe?"

Dana holstered her weapon and checked her bag for spare ammo. "Let's just see how the rest of today goes."

"Meaning if we're still alive tomorrow, we shop?" she asked, hoping to get a smile. Nothing. She sat up on the bed and tucked her feet underneath her. "Okay. What's up?"

"I'm in work mode."

"You're in grump mode."

Dana unzipped her suitcase. "Sylvio's men found you. We don't know how." She shrugged. "That makes me a little jumpy."

"I don't think that's why you're upset."

Dana reached inside her suitcase for some pajamas and headed to the bathroom. "Neither of us has slept in a while. Let's just get some rest and—"

"I gave Kyle his card back."

Dana hesitated in the bathroom doorway before turning to meet Chloe's gaze. "You don't owe me an explanation," she said. "I'll be out in a minute."

Taz trotted over and whined softly as he stared at the doorknob. Even he could sense something had changed between them.

Chloe's cell phone vibrated on the nightstand. She accepted the call and put it on speaker. "Hi, Maribel."

"Is Dana with you?"

"Of course. Why?"

A heavy silence crept on the line. "Sylvio posted bail about fifteen minutes ago."

CHAPTER FOURTEEN

Ice cold fingers traveled the length of Chloe's spine. "What judge would grant bail to that monster?"

Taz wagged his tail excitedly as Dana opened the bathroom door.

"At this point, our case boils down to your word against his," Maribel said, her tone curt.

"And the fact that I'm a cop with a solid record doesn't carry any weight?"

Maribel sighed. "The judge watched the recording."

Chloe couldn't bring herself to respond. She felt violated all over again.

"I'm sorry, Chloe. Legally, there was nothing I could do to stop it."

She took a deep breath. "Did the search warrant turn up anything?"

"No. This bastard's good at covering his tracks. We haven't been able to establish any connection between Sylvio and the shooters."

She could hear the frustration in Maribel's voice.

"What about the nurse I told you about," Dana asked, "the one who worked with Gabbi and saw Sylvio's tattoo? Was she able to make a positive ID?"

"We haven't been able to locate her. She never showed up for work yesterday."

Dana and Chloe stared at each other.

"Sylvio got to her," Chloe said finally.

Dana nodded. "He's tying up loose ends."

She turned her attention back to Maribel. "Let us help with the investigation—"

"You know I can't recommend that."

"Hold on," Chloe said. "Just think about it for a minute. I know how Sylvio's mind works better than anyone. Let us have a look at his house on the Vineyard. We can go there today and do a walk through with the local PD."

"Absolutely not. That would compromise the integrity of my case. There's a good chance the judge would exclude from trial any evidence you touched. Fruit of the poisonous tree."

"We could be anonymous consultants. Let the Tisbury PD get credit for discovery. We point them in the right direction and never touch anything."

"This isn't up for negotiation."

"But I'm the only one who's spent any time with Sylvio! My *specialty* is sex crimes. If I was backed against the wall like you right now, I'd sure as hell want me on my team." Taz leaped up on the bed and settled beside her, his ears perked in concern.

"As much as I do want that, I could never allow it. Chris Slater is a damn good criminal defense attorney—the best money can buy. I have no choice. That would be the end of our case."

"Fine. But give us *something* to do." Chloe brought her hands to her temples. "Other than bide our time until the next hit."

"That's exactly what I need the two of you to focus on right now—keeping yourselves safe. As far as we can tell, you're his only surviving victim, Chloe. Once a jury hears what he did to you, there's a good chance they'll convict based solely on your testimony. Sylvio knows that, which is why he's going all-out on the hit."

The thought of sharing every gory detail in a courtroom full of strangers made her feel sick to her stomach. What if they didn't believe her? What if they watched the video and decided it looked like she was enjoying herself?

"Chloe? You there?"

She let out her breath, feeling defeated. "I'm here."

"Have some faith in me," Maribel said, her tone softer. "Trust me. I want this bastard behind bars as much as you do. I'll do everything I can to make that happen."

They hung up. She set her phone back on the nightstand.

Dana sat on the bed across from her. "Walk me through that last day. The day Sylvio released you." Dark, knowing eyes met hers. "You haven't told me about that yet."

Chloe felt the lump in her throat and looked away.

"Maribel's at a dead end with the case. This is something we need to explore."

She took a deep breath and returned Dana's gaze. "What do you want to know?"

"Walk me through everything that happened the last day."

Long seconds ticked by in silence. Chloe shut her eyes and opened her mind to the memories she'd been fighting so hard to recover for the past two years—memories that had finally surfaced after Hunter died in the seat beside her.

"Sylvio stuck to the same schedule every day," she explained. "After he ate dinner at night, he'd unlock the door, handcuff me to the bed, and…" Unable to finish, she found it ironic that her job consisted mostly of getting victims to tell their stories. How could she ever look another victim in the eye if she couldn't even tell her own? She took a deep breath, tried again. "He raped me every night after he ate dinner."

Dana nodded. "There was evidence he raped the other three women repeatedly. So I'd assumed he did the same to you. I'm sorry, Chloe."

Taz scooted closer on the bed and set his head in her lap. They sat in silence as Chloe adjusted to the unwelcome memories of Sylvio having his way with her body.

"Did you and Sylvio have dinner together at night?"

"No."

"You said he assaulted you after he ate dinner. How do you know that?"

"Sylvio's a creature of habit. He smelled like peppers on Mondays, garlic on Tuesdays, Italian dressing on Wednesdays, fish on Thursdays, onions on Fridays, something cheesy...like Parmesan or Romano on Saturdays, and chocolate on Sundays." Sunday was probably the only day he splurged and ate dessert. Chloe guessed he spent hours each day at the gym. Every muscle in his body was sculpted with obsessive precision. "He kept to the same routine the last night I was there. The only difference was..." She trailed off, remembering.

"Was what?" Dana prompted.

"He was especially violent."

"Tell me what happened."

She shook her head. "I don't want to talk about this."

"I know," Dana said gently. "But I need you to try."

Chloe looked away and said nothing.

"You need to tell this to someone." Dana studied her for a moment, rose from the bed she was sitting on, and walked over to sit beside her. "We can chip away at this together. And if it needs to be a little at a time, that's okay. But you have to get all of it out, every ugly piece of it."

She knew Dana was right. If she ever hoped to rid herself of Sylvio completely, she needed to share everything. "He was like an animal that night," she said finally. "The rape was exceptionally brutal. He held nothing back." She let the memories run their course, vivid and searing. "It lasted for hours. My body went numb. I stopped fighting and just lay there. I didn't care what he did to me anymore." She shrugged, crying. "Eventually, he got bored and stopped. That's when he gave me a choice. I could either stay with him for another twenty-five days—after which he'd let me go free—or he could kill me that night and end my suffering once and for all."

"You chose to die," Dana said sadly.

"One of the easiest decisions I've ever made."

"Is that when he started beating you?" Dana asked, wiping the tears from her cheeks. "I saw the photos."

She nodded, stroking Taz. "He took the cuffs off and told me to fight back. First few blows hurt like hell. After that, I honestly didn't feel much of anything. I dropped to the floor, shut my eyes, and just waited for everything to be over."

Dana reached out, took her hand, and held it tightly between hers.

"The next thing I remember is waking up in the hospital, what turned out to be a week later."

"Someone found you in front of your old department, right?"

She nodded. "My old partner did. Just after midnight."

Dana stood and started pacing the room. Taz jumped down from the bed to join her. "If you had to guess, what time would you say Sylvio came into your room that night?"

"His usual time. Around seven."

"And how long did the assault last?"

"I don't know." Chloe shivered. It had felt like forever. "A few hours, maybe."

"Which would bring the time to about ten. So we can assume wherever he kept you was about two hours from the Tisbury police station." Dana stared at the carpet as she paced. "You said he was a creature of habit. Ate the same thing for dinner on certain days."

"Right. But how does that help us?"

"We could canvass the grocery stores within that two hour travel window. See if an employee recognizes him."

Chloe wasn't sure how that would help them find where she was held. The grocery store probably wouldn't have his address on file, but it was a start. One clue could lead to another. A ray of hope cut through the darkness of the past. "Just because Maribel doesn't want us officially on the case or touching evidence doesn't mean we can't dig around a little."

"These past few days have been very stressful." Dana stopped pacing and set her hands on her hips. "I'm thinking we could both use a little vacation. Someplace quiet and near the beach."

"Hmm." Chloe frowned, pretending to give the suggestion serious thought. "Well, the Vineyard's pretty quiet this time of year."

❖

Chloe was already asleep. Dana had taken the bed closest to the door. There was only a nightstand between them. She stared at the ceiling, wide awake. Knowing Chloe had chosen to die rather than face another twenty-five days in captivity broke her heart. It dawned on her that Sylvio had probably given the other victims the same ultimatum. Her heart broke for them, too. Since all four women had been imprisoned by him for the same amount of time, it seemed they had all made the same choice.

Despite her best efforts to quiet her mind and get some sleep, her thoughts kept returning to her wife. Gabbi had been so full of light and love. Definitely a glass-half-full person, she was one of the most optimistic people Dana had ever encountered—which made knowing she might have chosen to die even more gut-wrenching. A part of her still couldn't believe she was gone.

If Sylvio hadn't cut his finger and shown up at the ER that day, Gabbi would still be here. They would've celebrated their child's third birthday in June. Gabbi would no doubt be pregnant by now with their second baby.

Careful not to make a sound, she turned on her side away from Chloe and let the tears fall into her pillow. Her sweet Gabbi had suffered and died at the hands of a sociopath. How would she ever be able to come to terms with that?

Before she knew it, Chloe was slipping underneath the covers behind her. Without a word, she pressed her body against Dana's and held her as she cried.

❖

Taz leaned against Chloe's leg as she gazed out the window of the rental car center. The familiar scents of seawater and sand welcomed her home. It felt strange to be back.

Having signed the last of the paperwork, Dana stepped away from the counter and held out the keys. "You know your way around here better than I do."

Chloe led the way through the parking lot and stopped short, double-checking to make sure the parking space number matched the one on the keychain. "You rented a convertible?"

"We're supposed to be on vacation."

"But it's too cold to put the top down."

"When I drive a convertible, I feel rebellious." Dana shrugged. "I need to feel like a rebel if I'm about to break the rules."

They all climbed in. Chloe wondered how Maribel would react when she found out about their trip. She started the engine and glanced at her watch: two fifty-five p.m. She put the car in gear. "Hungry?" They hadn't eaten all day. They'd driven straight from Ogunquit to catch the ferry to Martha's Vineyard.

"Starving. How does it feel to be back?"

"I don't know," she said. "Different, I guess." Chloe slipped her sunglasses on. It was a beautiful day. Chilly, but the sun was out. Even though she'd only been gone a year, it felt a lot longer. Hadn't she vowed never to set foot here again? She took a deep breath, thankful Dana was there beside her. "Let's get a late lunch. I know just the place."

They drove to a restaurant on the beach and ordered lobster rolls to go. She looked down at Taz. "Don't worry," she told him as he sniffed the bag in her hands. "I got one for you, too."

She led the way along the sandy pavement to a spot she knew all too well. She slipped off her shoes and socks, stuffed her socks inside her sneakers, and carried them by the laces when the paved walkway ended. Dana did the same. Cold sand filled the spaces between her toes.

Taz barked at some seagulls a short distance away. He peered up at her and whined, as if asking permission to chase them. Chloe took a good look around. The beach was deserted. "Go ahead," she said, unclipping his leash. "Don't wander too far."

Dana pointed behind them. "The sign we just passed says *Private Property.*"

"I know." Chloe kept walking. The ocean rekindled her senses. Smiling, she watched as a fisherman cast his line from the pier up ahead, his face stern and unyielding. He looked just the same as she remembered. Seagulls swooped high overhead and cried out with envy as he reeled in his catch. With experienced hands, he grabbed the line, unhooked a striped bass, and tossed it into a green bucket.

He cast his eyes on Chloe as they approached. "I'd say Boston agrees with you, Cagney." He tipped the brim of his fishing hat toward her.

"And I'd say retirement agrees with you." She stood on tiptoe to give him a peck on the cheek and then stepped aside to make introductions. "Charlie, this is Dana Blake."

"Nice to meet you." Dana wisely refrained from shaking his hand.

"And that's Taz," she said, pointing to the sopping wet German shepherd as he dragged a giant blue crab from the surf. The two were now engaged in a serious stare down.

Charlie raised an eyebrow before returning his attention to Dana. "You wouldn't be Johnny's daughter, by any chance?"

Dana nodded. "You knew him?"

"Sure did. We fished some together, back in the day." He looked back and forth between them. "You two don't remember?"

"Remember what?" Chloe asked, still trying to wrap her brain around the uncanny coincidence.

"The two of you met when you were nine, Cagney. Spent a few weekends on the boat with us that summer. You were like two peas in a pod back then."

"I *knew* I had seen you somewhere before!" Dana said, regarding Chloe with a look of wonder. "But for the life of me, I couldn't figure out where."

Chloe thought back to a summer of fun on the boat with a friend about her age. "Your dad...he called you *Dee*," she said, finally making the connection.

Dana laughed. "He never called me by my first name unless I was in trouble."

"Good to see you after all these years, Dee." He glanced at the paper bag in Chloe's hand. "Go eat your lobster rolls. I'll have your room ready by the time you get back." He set the fishing rod aside and started packing up.

She reached out for Dana's hand and led her toward the end of the pier.

Seagulls circled overhead and finally dispersed, voicing their complaints that the fisherman was calling it a day. Steady, soothing waves lapped at the shore behind them. The sun would be setting in another hour or so. Perfect. Chloe sat and dangled her feet over the edge.

"Can you believe we knew each other when we were kids?" She wondered if that explained the connection she'd felt with Dana from the moment they'd met at the café.

"I never would've remembered if Charlie hadn't reminded me. We had so much fun together that summer." Dana looked over at her. "Your last name is Maddox. Why did Charlie call you Cagney?"

"Christine Cagney,'" she said, reminding Dana of the TV show that set her on the path to becoming a cop. "Charlie's nickname for me since I was ten." She took a bite of the lobster roll. It was every bit as good as she remembered. "He raised me after my dad died."

Dana took a bite and rolled her eyes. "Oh my God. This is delicious," she said, still chewing. "How old were you when he died?"

"Eight. Liver cancer."

"I'm sorry." Dana took another bite. "Is Charlie your uncle?"

She shook her head. "He and my dad went to the academy together. They worked the same beat for fifteen years."

"You didn't tell me your dad was a cop."

Chloe playfully bumped Dana's shoulder. "You didn't ask."

"What about your mom? Where's she?"

"Drugs. She left when I was six."

"I'm sorry." Dana reached over and gave Chloe's leg a gentle squeeze.

"Old news." Chloe had spent her childhood and teenage years wondering if she'd done something to make her mother leave. She'd seen too many people lose the battle against addiction in the time since to continue blaming herself, but her heart still carried the scars.

Chloe stared out at the ocean and scooted closer to Dana. They finished eating and watched the sunset, holding hands.

CHAPTER FIFTEEN

The light was fading as they made their way back down the pier, hand in hand. Dana couldn't help but smile. It felt wonderful to hold hands with a woman she knew she was falling for. With her belly full and evening upon them, she felt exhaustion starting to seep in around the edges of her mind.

Dana wasn't quite sure what to expect with tonight's sleeping arrangements. She wanted nothing more than to be intimate with the incredible woman beside her, but she also recognized the importance of waiting until the time was right for both of them. How would it feel to make love to someone other than Gabbi? After four years, she felt herself approaching a point where she was finally ready to find out.

But she couldn't say the same for Chloe. She had no idea how long it would take for Chloe to feel comfortable enough to share her body. She was *gorgeous*. There was no denying that. But she had been violated in ways Dana could only imagine, and it probably left her feeling vulnerable, untrusting, less than beautiful, and maybe even ashamed. Dana was prepared to go slow and steady, never pushing, never asking for more than Chloe was ready to give.

Taz suddenly bounded toward them, yelping in pain. The giant blue crab from earlier was dangling from his upper lip. With a viselike grip, said crab appeared the unlikely victor in the battle of teeth against claws.

Dana lifted the crab by its rear legs to help ease the weight on Taz's lip. It was locked on pretty tight, and she had no idea how to get it off. She and Chloe knelt beside the duo to examine the crab's blue pincer.

Taz's cries were deafening. It was hard to believe this was the same dog who bravely confronted an armed assailant without batting an eye. "Man up," Dana said, fearing a ruptured eardrum was imminent.

He looked back at her and stopped wailing just long enough to growl.

"Should we shoot it?" Dana asked, her hand moving to the holster on her hip.

"Let's get them in the water. It'll let go there." Chloe stood and started leading Taz to the surf.

Following Chloe's lead, Dana waded into the freezing water. Taz cried louder and tried to back away. Scared and in pain, he obviously didn't understand what they were doing.

Chloe leaned over and looked him in the eye. "Put your face in the water, Taz. Trust me."

To Dana's astonishment, he submerged his head underwater without hesitation. The crab immediately released its grip and disappeared along the ocean floor. When he lifted his head from the water, his lip was finally crab-free.

Chloe rinsed his bloodied lip with seawater and whispered soothingly in his ear. "Man up?" she said, rolling her eyes at Dana. "I'll try that when *you* have a crab the size of a dinner plate hanging off your face."

Dana shrugged and laughed at her own expense. "That's what my dad always said when I got hurt." Back on the beach, she knelt in the sand and offered Taz a heartfelt apology. Fortunately for her, he didn't appear to hold a grudge and readily forgave her with a sloppy wet kiss.

❖

"I don't understand," Dana said, taking a seat on the gray armchair in their bedroom. "There are two guest rooms in this house, but Charlie put us together."

Chloe turned down the plush comforter and switched off the bedside lamp. A seashell night-light illuminated Dana's silhouette in the dark. "And?"

"And there's only one bed." Dana looked cute in the football jersey she was wearing as pajamas. "Is this his way of telling me to go find a hotel?"

"No," Chloe laughed. "It's his way of telling you he thinks we're sleeping together."

Dana froze. "You're joking."

"Charlie knows I've brought only one other person to the end of the pier for a lobster roll."

"Michael?"

She nodded and sat on the ottoman facing Dana.

"But how does Charlie know?" Dana asked. "I could be a completely platonic friend."

"Charlie figures things out fast, which is exactly what made him a good cop." She frowned. "It sucked going through my teen years with him. I couldn't get away with anything."

Dana was quiet for a moment. "So the lobster roll is the deal cincher?"

"Yep." Chloe leaned forward, brushing her lips against Dana's. The lips that met hers were soft and so gentle. Dana's tongue flicked over hers just briefly and set her body on fire. She stood and led Dana to the bed. "You okay with Charlie knowing about us?"

"Maybe I should be the one asking you that question."

They both climbed under the sheets as she thought about it. "Charlie has never judged me on anything in my life," she said honestly. "He just wants me to be happy."

Dana lay on her back and extended her arm as an open invitation to snuggle. Chloe settled right in. It didn't escape her attention that their bodies fit together perfectly. She wrapped an arm around Dana's hips and pulled her closer. She smelled like soap and fabric softener. She pressed her bare legs against Dana's, their warmth and softness a welcome change to the coarse, hairy legs of a man.

Chloe looked forward to the day when she could share herself intimately with Dana. She didn't know when that would be, but she had an inkling it would be soon. Despite her recently recovered memories of Sylvio, she felt her mind and body opening up to the idea of making love again. Dana's touch ignited a fire in Chloe totally different from any partner she'd had before.

Dana kissed her on the forehead and gave her a gentle squeeze. She felt…safe with Dana, comfortable in Dana's respect for her need to take things slowly. They had faced a lot together in such a short amount of time. In many ways, it felt like they were already an established couple. Chloe looked forward to exploring sex in a relationship where the intimacy transcended any she had known before.

Exhausted, she closed her eyes and nodded off, content in Dana's protective embrace.

❖

They awoke the next morning with a knock at the door. "Rise and shine!" Charlie called out from the other side. "Pancakes are on the griddle, Cagney."

Chloe smiled against Dana's neck and snuggled closer. "Charlie makes the best pancakes."

Dana stroked her back. "What time is it?"

"Early." The sun wasn't even up yet. "Forgot to mention Charlie doesn't believe in sleeping past five." Chloe switched on the bedside lamp. "Notice"—she waved her hand over the nightstand—"no alarm clock."

"Does Charlie believe in sharing pancakes with Cagney's roommate?"

She laughed, climbing out of bed to throw on some jeans. "I'll put in a good word."

Twenty minutes later, they were sitting around the kitchen table and watching the sunrise through enormous bay windows. Charlie sipped his coffee from a dark blue Fish Fear Me mug that Chloe had given him when she was nine. It was nice to see some things never changed.

"So, Dee," Charlie said, taking a stab at his pancake, "you're a cop."

Dana nodded. "Detective with the BPD."

"Oh, yeah?" He chewed. "Which department?"

Dana met Chloe's eyes and quickly looked away. "Family Justice."

"Ah. Sex crimes," he said, nodding. "I see."

Chloe held her breath, unsure how much of the puzzle Charlie had put together in her absence. She'd never told him what happened—only that Michael was murdered by an unidentified assailant. Two years ago, she'd waited until all of her bruises and broken bones were healed before she had allowed Charlie to see her.

He stuffed another forkful of pancake in his mouth, chewed, swallowed. "You gonna find the bastard that raped my Cagney?"

Chloe knocked over her chair in her haste to stand up. How could she have been so stupid to think she'd be able to keep something like that from Charlie?

Fork halfway to his mouth, he froze, watching her.

"Excuse me," she muttered. She hurried to the bathroom and barely made it to the toilet in time as her stomach rid itself of breakfast. She rinsed her mouth and leaned against the sink.

How could he have known this whole time and not told her? Was he trying to respect her privacy? She and Charlie had always been close, even before her dad died. Charlie hadn't replaced her dad exactly, but he was a damn close match. Why hadn't he reached out to her about this over the last two years? Charlie called her to check in every few days but never once did he bring up what happened.

Her next thought made her heart feel like it was being squeezed right out of her chest. Was he ashamed of her? She was a cop, after all, and she hadn't even been able to protect herself. Did he fault her for that?

A soft knock sounded at the door. "Cagney?"

She couldn't do this. Not here. Not now. No way. Facing Charlie was totally out of the question. "I need some time, Charlie."

He cracked the door open. "And what...two years isn't enough?"

"Leave this alone," she warned, stepping forward with the intent to leave.

He didn't move aside to let her pass.

Unable to meet his eyes, she stared at the floor, seething. "Get out of my way, Charlie."

"If that's what you want." He stepped aside. "But I hope you'll talk to me."

Chloe braced herself and met his eyes, expecting to see an accusation of weakness from one cop to another...judgment, scorn, blame, even shame. What she saw, instead, surprised her. Tears. She'd never seen this man cry. Not once in all the time she'd known him. She felt her chin start to quiver.

"So many times I wanted to talk to you about this, Cagney, but I was afraid you'd shut me out along with everyone else. I didn't want to lose you. I hoped eventually you'd come around and open up to me, when you were ready."

She nodded and stepped into his arms, feeling like she was eight again and had just lost her dad. Charlie had been there for her then, too. He had always been there. He was safe, comfortable, and familiar. Just the smell of him felt like home.

❖

Chloe sat beside Dana on the living room sofa as Charlie refilled their mugs with coffee and settled in the worn leather armchair across from them. He sipped at his coffee but said nothing, his forehead wrinkled in thought.

They'd already caught him up on the events to date: seeing Sylvio at the station, getting shot at by the sniper outside Chloe's condo, attending Sylvio's arraignment and seeing his tie, losing Hunter to the gunmen on her way to Vermont. Lastly—reluctantly—she told him about the video Sylvio had made of her.

Chloe followed his gaze as he studied Dana. "Why do I get the feeling this is personal for you?" he asked.

Dana didn't flinch. "Sylvio abducted and murdered my wife, Gabriela."

"I'm sorry," was all he offered as he dropped his gaze. He set his mug on the coffee table, laced his fingers together, and raised an eyebrow. "What's your game plan, Cagney?"

She knew that look. She'd seen it too many times in the past. Charlie had something up his sleeve. "We think the place where Sylvio kept me is about two hours from the Vineyard. Dana thinks it might pay off to canvass grocery stores within that two-hour travel window and see if anyone recognizes him."

"You saying you want to bring this to trial?" Charlie leaned forward. "To testify against him?"

Slowly, she nodded. "I have no other choice. He can't be allowed to do this to anyone else."

He narrowed his eyes. "There are other ways to handle men like Sylvio." He stared at her long and hard, his eyes unreadable.

She didn't—couldn't—look away. She knew exactly what Charlie was doing. He was letting his words sink in, allowing her the chance to accept his offer: terminate Sylvio to save her from having to testify in court.

She thought about it for a few moments and finally shook her head, adamant. "I won't give him the easy way out. He needs to pay for what he did by going to prison for the rest of his life."

Charlie rolled his shoulders. "C'mon," he said, standing. "Something I need to show you."

He led them to what she remembered as the workout room on the second floor. He'd pushed all of the equipment in one corner to make room for a desk, printer, police scanner, and a large map of the Vineyard and surrounding islands. A massive dry-erase board took up the length of one wall, detailing a timeline of some sort with endless notes scribbled in Charlie's small, neat print. The name Sylvio Caprazzio appeared in bold red letters at the top of the board.

Chloe's eyes wandered to a list of names on one side—all of them women, she noted, stepping closer. The first woman went missing on November 12, two decades ago. Personal details were written alongside each name. One name stood out. Gabriela Santos.

Her own name was at the bottom of the list. According to the board, she was, indeed, the only victim who'd survived.

She turned to face Charlie. "How long have you been looking into this?"

"Started digging around about eighteen months ago. Unofficially, of course." Charlie had retired several years ago.

"Why didn't you tell me?"

"Heard through the grapevine you couldn't remember anything about your abduction. I knew those memories would surface sooner or later. They always do." Charlie sat on the edge of the desk. "I didn't want my investigation to taint your recollection of events."

Chloe turned back to the notes on the board. She stepped closer, squinting to make out the tiny print in the bottom left corner. *Sylvio Caprazzio, alias Donovan Marchante, signed ninety-nine year lease for Naushon Island on 3/15/1996.*

Just north of Martha's Vineyard and only accessible by boat, Naushon Island was seven miles long—the largest of the Elizabeth Islands. Chloe could hardly believe her eyes. Sylvio had obtained an entire island to ensure he had the seclusion and privacy needed to carry out his crimes. She watched as Dana's eyes zoomed in on the same spot.

"Just a stab in the dark here," Dana said, glancing up. "But is Naushon Island about two hours from Martha's Vineyard?"

"It is by boat," Charlie said.

CHAPTER SIXTEEN

You two are where?" Maribel shouted. Speakerphone was turned up to full volume on the cell. Dana and Chloe both took a step back.

"It was Dana's idea," Chloe blurted.

Dana stared at her. Her mouth hung open.

"When the hell did you get there?"

"Last night," they replied in unison.

"Please tell me you two haven't done anything to mess up my case."

Chloe stepped forward. "That's why we're calling—"

"Because you messed up my case?"

"No—"

"Because you're determined to give me a migraine two hours before my alarm even goes off?"

Chloe cleared her throat. "Not at all." She realized she was in over her head and looked beseechingly to Dana. But Dana ran a thumb and forefinger over her own mouth and threw away the imaginary key. Chloe was on her own.

"Well, then"—Maribel went on, growing louder by the second—"it better be because your lives are in peril and you're calling to give me your last will and testament."

Chloe frowned. "Um…no."

"Too bad! Because that's the only thing that would've gotten you both off the hook."

Dana finally took pity on her, pretended to stick a large piece of tape over Chloe's mouth, and courageously stepped closer to the phone. "We're pretty sure we've located Sylvio's hideout. We think it's where he kept his victims."

Silence. "Fill me in." Maribel sounded a tad less angry.

Dana told her about Charlie and the investigation he'd launched on Chloe's behalf. She explained that Sylvio had leased Naushon Island under an alias. "According to Charlie, there are nine victims total—all female. But he thinks there could be more."

"My God." Stunned silence crept on the line. "Did any of the others survive?"

Dana reached over and held Chloe's hand. "No."

Maribel said she'd make arrangements for a search warrant of the property on Naushon Island. "Assuming we find a dwelling, I'll want you to do a walk through to confirm it's where you were held during the time in question."

The thought of setting foot in that place again made her grow suddenly cold. She looked to Dana, a knot of dread in her stomach.

"We'll take it a step at a time," Dana assured her. "And I'll be there beside you the whole way through."

❖

Charlie coasted in and tethered his speedboat to the long pier on Naushon Island. "You sure you don't want me to tag along?" he asked as she and Dana climbed out.

Chloe shook her head and gave Taz the command to stay. As much as she wanted Taz with her right now, he wouldn't be allowed inside the house due to possible crime scene contamination. "Wait here," she told Charlie. "I'm hoping this won't take long."

"Roger that." He grabbed his fishing pole, baited the hook, and cast his line before they made it to the end of the pier.

She realized the past two years must have been difficult for Charlie. Knowing what had happened to her and keeping quiet about it took a kind of strength she couldn't fathom. She knew she was like a daughter to him. He'd never had kids of his own. He'd devoted his life to being the best role model he could be and raising her in her dad's absence. She wished she had confided in Charlie a lot sooner. Shutting him out was a mistake she now deeply regretted. He deserved better than that.

A uniformed officer from the local police department met them near the end of the pier. She was grateful it wasn't someone from her old department. She didn't think she could handle a familiar face right now.

He reached out to introduce himself, first to Dana and then to Chloe. "Sergeant Rilkes," he said. "But everyone just calls me Bill." His thick hair, bleached blond by the sun, was growing in several shades darker at the roots. With a sun-parched face and a fading tan from summer, he was probably younger than he looked. His time on the islands had no doubt aged him. "The cabin we found is in the center of the island," he told them. "It's about a three-mile trek. Since there aren't any paved roads on the island, we ferried these golf carts over as a more efficient means of transport." He led them to a black and white golf cart with the department's insignia on the side and rear panels. He hopped in and started the engine.

Chloe was glad she and Dana had worn their winter coats. They stuffed their hands inside their pockets to keep warm as cold ocean winds assaulted them from all directions.

"Here we are." Rilkes parked a short distance away from the cabin and stepped down from the golf cart. "Take your time. I'll meet you inside whenever you're ready."

Dana studied her. "Want to take a walk and get some fresh air before we go inside?"

Chloe gathered some unruly curls and tucked them back into her ponytail. "We just rode in a golf cart. Believe me when I say, I've gotten all the air I'll ever need." She reached over and gave Dana's arm a gentle squeeze. "I just want to get this over with."

Sparse island vegetation grew as far as the eye could see. This was definitely remote—perfect for what Sylvio must have had in mind when he secured the property. No one else lived on the island. She knew from Charlie's research that Naushon Island was privately owned but maintained by a trust. Charlie had downloaded some historic aerial photos he'd found online. The island she was standing on looked nothing at all like those photos. Gorgeous mansions with pristine yards once stood here. Someone had obviously demolished those houses and erected a simple rustic cabin in their place.

Her hands grew moist as they approached the cabin. The wood was weathered, the land wild and overgrown. Even though Sylvio had drugged her before entering and then beaten her unconscious before leaving, Chloe knew this was the place. Something about it felt sickeningly familiar.

The cabin's screen door opened, and a familiar face stepped outside. As usual, Maribel was dressed to kill in a power suit and high heels, her red woolen peacoat neatly folded over one arm. "I've already been inside," she said. "From everything you described, it looks like this is the place." She held the screen door ajar.

Chloe was just a few steps inside when Sylvio's cologne hit her. It took every ounce of willpower not to turn and run out.

The living room was sparsely furnished. A black leather sofa and metal coffee table faced a huge flat screen TV. A small dining nook off an even smaller kitchen held a folding table with one chair.

Maribel stepped in front of her. "This way," she said, leading them to a large pantry. Inside was a formidable looking door that was guarded by a baby-faced cop. Lean and freckled, he tipped the brim of his hat as they passed.

The cement staircase seemed to go on forever. It smelled damp and raw as they descended farther. The temperature had dropped substantially by the time they reached the bottom. Chloe shivered. She was always cold down here.

Maribel led them to a second door. "There were eight combination locks on this door alone," she said, pointing to the severed locks piled in one corner. She grabbed a flashlight off a nearby shelf, pressed her hand to the door handle, and turned back to Chloe. "It's pitch black in here. There are six bedrooms off the main tunnel, each one slightly different than—"

"Six?" Chloe interrupted, panic clawing at her chest.

"There's nothing to be afraid of. I'll be in front of you the whole time," Maribel said, taking her hand.

"And I'll be right behind you," Dana said, taking her other hand.

"I know this is hard. After today, you'll never have to come back here again," Maribel promised.

Chloe nodded. "Let's just get it over with."

Maribel handed her the flashlight because she needed both hands to pry open the heavy door. A whoosh of cold dank air blasted over them, carrying with it the stench of the collective fear of Sylvio's brutalized victims. Maribel held the flashlight in one hand and Chloe's hand in the other as she led her into the depths of hell.

The sound of Maribel's heels clicking on the cement floor echoed off the tunnel walls. Chloe heard her own heart pounding in her ears. Her arms and legs broke out in goose bumps as much from fear as from the chill in the air.

The first bedroom they came to initially seemed identical in every way to the one where she had been held. It had all the same furniture and accessories—right down to the solid beige comforter on the bed—but it was slightly smaller than the room that had been her prison. "This isn't it," she said, retreating into the tunnel for a look at bedroom number two.

They'd already made it through four of the six bedrooms when the beam of the flashlight swept across a curtain mounted over an open doorway. Maribel walked right past it, her heels clicking in the darkness.

"What's this?" Chloe asked, halting in front of the curtain.

"Sylvio used that room as storage space." Maribel pointed the flashlight at the floor. "Trust me, Chloe, you don't want to go in there."

But she had an overwhelming urge to step inside. She pointed at the flashlight. "Can I borrow that?"

In an obvious effort to dissuade her from entering, Maribel made no motion to relinquish the flashlight. Chloe withdrew her cell phone and activated the flashlight feature. She pushed the curtain aside and stepped in, with Dana and Maribel close on her heels.

She found a light switch to the left of the doorway and flipped it on. The shelves were filled with meticulously folded lingerie. A variety of sadomasochistic devices dangled from hooks in the ceiling, their black leather straps ugly, mean, and daunting. Framed photos of naked women hung on one wall. From the haunted looks in their eyes, Chloe guessed they were Sylvio's victims. She examined the photos more closely. Sylvio's signature was at the bottom of each one. He'd also taken the liberty of labeling them with a number and a date, like a grotesque artist signing and numbering prints in a series.

She worked her way down the wall, studying the women in the photos. Not out of curiosity. She did it out of respect for them. Bearing witness to their suffering was the least she could do. Turning away from them now would be like leaving them to suffer all alone.

There were so many women.

She burned each of their faces to memory. Black, white, Chinese, Hispanic…tall, short, athletic, voluptuous. Aside from the fact they were all beautiful and female, there seemed to be no common denominator to the faces and bodies before her.

Chloe put her hand to her mouth as tears ran down her cheeks. These women were barely alive by the time Sylvio had finished with them. She prayed Sylvio's wasn't the last face they saw. She hoped they'd all had a chance to see their loved ones in the hospital one last time before they died.

Her own photo was last. She remembered the photo session in vivid detail. Sylvio had instructed her on the ways he wanted her to pose. The shame she felt as he snapped each photo welled up from that long-forgotten place. Signed and dated in the bottom right-hand corner, she was dubbed, quite simply, *Number 11*.

"There were eleven victims," she said aloud, unable to grasp the fact that ten women had gone before her.

Dana and Maribel joined her. She watched Dana's face as she examined Gabbi's photo, her eyes filling with tears. Beautiful Gabriela was Sylvio's tenth victim. Now they knew for sure.

She slipped her hand inside Dana's and stood beside her, their shoulders touching. Long seconds stretched into minutes. Neither she nor Maribel made an attempt to lure Dana away. Chloe sensed she needed this time to process…to grieve.

"What will happen to these photos?" Chloe finally asked, directing her gaze at Maribel.

"Once we confirm the identity of each victim, these photos will be entered as evidence at Sylvio's trial."

"And what will happen to them after the trial's over?"

"They'll be copied and digitally stored. The originals will probably be destroyed at some point."

"Can I have them?"

"You want your photo?" Maribel asked with a look of bewilderment.

"No," she said. "I want all of them—mine, Gabbi's, and the other women on this wall. They've been locked away all alone down here. They shouldn't be alone anymore. Someone needs to give them closure."

Dana wiped her cheeks with the back of one sleeve. Nodding, she squeezed Chloe's hand. "We want to take them with us. All of them." She finally looked away from Gabbi's photo to lock eyes with Maribel. "Promise me you'll make sure we get them when you're done."

Maribel nodded. "You have my word."

Step by step, they made their way down the tunnel to the two remaining bedrooms.

Chloe held tight to Dana's hand. Maribel turned the doorknob to enter bedroom number five. As the door swung open, the first wave of air washed over her. "This is it."

"Are you sure?" Dana asked.

"I marked off each day with my fingernail." She walked around the bed to the nightstand on the other side and slid the drawer open. "There, in the wood," she said, pointing. Centimeter-long scratches were lined up like marching soldiers along the inside of the drawer.

Dana bent down to have a closer look. "Twenty-five marks for twenty-five days," she said sadly, running her fingertips over the scarred surface. She looked around the room. "There aren't any windows or clocks in here. How'd you keep track of time?"

Chloe motioned to the light switch above Maribel's shoulder. "Turn the light off." As she did, a tiny sliver of sunlight penetrated the darkness from a hairline crack in the ceiling. "That's how," she said, her voice quivering.

Dana's hand found hers as Maribel flipped the switch and forced the darkness into submission once again.

Chloe made the mistake of looking up. She caught her reflection in the ceiling mirror. *Look up,* he'd whispered in her ear one night. *Watch what I'm doing. I own you—*

"Chloe?" Dana's voice sounded far away. "You okay?"

She pushed past Dana as the walls and ceiling bore down on her. She felt like she was going to be sick as she made her way through the tunnel and up the stairs once again.

Chloe threw open the screen door, descended the porch steps, and jogged across the sandy lot. Dana was just a few steps behind her. She leaned against the golf cart and scanned the front porch for Maribel.

Where the hell is Maribel? she wondered, her stomach in knots. A full minute passed with no sign of her. Chloe felt her panic rising to the surface like a recently shaken carbonated beverage. Maribel was in Sylvio's clutches. Downstairs. In the tunnel. Locked inside that very same bedroom. He must have been hiding in a secret chamber somewhere, closing and locking her in before she had the chance to escape.

How could she have left Maribel behind like that? She was just about to tell Dana they needed to go back when the screen door swung open. Maribel stepped onto the porch.

Chloe hadn't realized she was holding her breath. She exhaled with one big sigh of relief and watched as Maribel negotiated the sand in high heels. Of course, she thought, logic returning to her world. Maribel wasn't locked away in the tunnel. She just took longer climbing out of there because of her poor choice in shoes.

"I'm sorry," Chloe said, shaking her head. "I couldn't stay down there another second."

Maribel set a hand on her shoulder, her brown eyes uncharacteristically soft and unguarded. "You did amazing." She turned to Dana. "Why don't the two of you head back to

Charlie's? I'll have everything wrapped up here by this evening. Let's meet for dinner. I'll have more information by then."

"Why don't we just wait for you?" Dana suggested. "You can ride back with us on the boat."

"No, you two go. I'll catch up with you later."

Chloe frowned. "I'd feel better if we waited—"

"I'll be fine," Maribel said, dismissing them with a wave of her well-manicured hand. She leaned in for a quick hug. "I'll take the three of you to dinner tonight. I'd like to meet Charlie and thank him in person."

Chloe sent her a text with Charlie's address and watched as Maribel stepped into the lion's den once again.

CHAPTER SEVENTEEN

Chloe gestured to the empty golf cart. "Sergeant Rilkes must still be inside. Mind if we walk back?" She figured the fresh air would do them both good. It would also give them time to leave the cabin—and all of its contents—behind.

They walked the first few minutes in silence. The smell of seawater and the rhythmic sound of lapping waves instantly calmed her. She found it ironic that such a beautiful place could harbor such a terrible secret for so long.

"Want to talk about it?" Dana asked without taking her eyes from the sandy path before them.

"No." She shook her head. "Not yet." There were so many painful memories swimming around in her head. It was hard to pinpoint just one—even harder to talk coherently about it. Everything was still a mix of raw emotion.

Walking, she thought about the photos. Seeing Gabbi's must have been a shock for Dana. "I'm sorry you had to see Gabbi like that."

"I'm not," Dana said without hesitating. "Knowing what Gabbi faced at the end of her life is better than not knowing. Even though she's dead, knowing what she went through means she's not alone anymore. Now she has a voice." She met Chloe's gaze. "You're her voice, Chloe. You're the voice for all those women."

She nodded. Dana was right. She suddenly found herself looking forward to testifying against Sylvio. She'd be honoring all the women in those photos by taking the stand, without fear and without embarrassment or shame. Since none of the others were here to tell what happened to them, she would tell their story for them. She would be their voice.

Feeling empowered for the first time in two years, she held Dana's hand all the way back to the boat.

❖

Charlie dropped them off at his pier and announced he was heading out to sea for a few more hours of fishing. Chloe got the feeling he was giving them some time alone. He was quiet on the boat ride back. He didn't bombard her with questions like most fathers in his position would. That's one of the things she loved about him. Eternally patient and self-disciplined, he always knew when to set his curiosity aside and just let her be.

Taz watched with his satellite dish ears at full attention as she and Dana climbed down from the boat. Remaining at Charlie's side, he made no move to join them on the pier.

"It's subtle, but I'm getting the feeling you'd like to go fishing, too," she said to Taz.

He cocked his head at her and then looked up at Charlie, as if asking for permission to tag along.

"Of course you can come," Charlie replied, readily picking up on Taz's expression of desperation and hope.

Chloe watched as the two boys sped away from the island. She turned to Dana. "Taz is so relaxed and happy now. It feels like something's changed with him."

"Back at the station, Fred said he was a hero." Dana shook her head in disbelief. "Call me crazy, but I swear Taz understood. He's been a different dog ever since."

Chloe smiled. She was glad to know the other people around her were starting to see Taz for who he really was. He was special. No doubt about that. Taz was truly one of a kind.

They walked back to Charlie's and warmed up with some Earl Grey tea—Chloe's favorite. Still feeling chilled to the bone from the boat ride home, they decided to shower before dinner. Chloe went first. She lathered up and let the hot water rinse away all traces of the cabin. Renewed and recharged, she wrapped herself in a towel and stepped out from the bathroom to let Dana have a turn.

Holding the towel against her body, she sat on the bed as Dana showered. She thought long and hard about what she wanted from Dana and about what she was ready to give in return. By the time she heard the water shut off in the bathroom, she'd made up her mind.

Steam drifted into the bedroom as Dana opened the bathroom door. She looked over at Chloe on the bed, still in her towel. "Are you having a fashion crisis?" she asked with an amused grin. "Trying to decide what to wear to dinner tonight?" Dana's clothes were already neatly laid out on a chair in the corner.

Chloe shook her head. "I know what I'm wearing." She stood and lowered the blinds on the windows. Without a light on, the room fell into a comfortable darkness. She stepped over to Dana in her bare feet, took her hand, and led her to the bed.

Still wrapped in a towel, Dana searched her face, her dark eyes gentle and curious. "When I said we could take things slow, I meant it," Dana whispered. "You don't have to do this, Chloe."

"I know." Undaunted, she kissed her way along Dana's collarbone, up to her ear, along the curve of her jaw, and over to her lips, diving into her mouth with a need that felt primal, insatiable. She felt Dana's mouth respond to hers, matching her own need for release. Chloe pulled back, breathing hard as she met Dana's eyes.

A thin gold chain hung from Dana's neck, the tiny heart-shaped charm tucked in the crevice of her collarbone. Dana was toned and athletic, her skin soft and unblemished. She traced Dana's neckline with her fingertips and gradually made her way down to the top of the towel.

Dana didn't resist as Chloe loosened the towel and let it drop to the floor. Chloe did the same with hers, allowing them to bring their bodies together for the first time, skin to skin. She felt Dana's breasts against hers as Dana probed inside her mouth, using her tongue in ways none of her previous lovers ever had.

Chloe held nothing back as she returned the favor, slipping into Dana's mouth in a rhythm so seductive she couldn't help but wonder what their tongues would feel like in other places.

"Are you sure this is what you want?" Dana asked, pulling back.

Chloe nodded and wondered for the first time if maybe Dana was the one who wasn't ready.

As if in answer to her question, Dana lowered her gently to the bed and eased her body over the top of Chloe's. Their tongues danced more feverishly than ever. Her need was building with every caress. Part of her could hardly believe she was about to make love to this incredible woman.

The steady throbbing at her core quickly turned from mildly pleasant to downright uncomfortable. Dana kissed the scars on her breasts, straddled her thigh, and brought her lips to Chloe's for a slow sweet kiss. She paused and searched Chloe's face.

There it was—the look that made her think Dana knew all her deepest secrets and fears. Eyes that cut straight to her soul.

Seemingly satisfied that Chloe wasn't backing down, Dana guided her inside as her fingers explored Chloe's depths. Dana's silky dark hair, still wet from her recent shower, fanned out over her shoulders. Sweat streamed from their bodies as they ground wildly against one another.

Finally, their eyes locked. Chloe was on the edge.

"Don't look away," Dana said. "Stay with me, Chloe."

She held on to Dana's gaze the whole time. Their soft cries cut through the air as they climaxed in unison. She felt the aftershocks against her fingers, certain Dana was feeling the same inside her. Without the need for words, they shifted into a calmer rhythm, hips rocking back and forth in an intuitive understanding of needing a gentle, unhurried touch. It was the most intimate connection she'd ever shared with anyone in her life.

Dana kissed her slowly, tenderly. They stared at one another, the intimacy too deep to spoil with words. Dana's touch had finally cleansed her body.

❖

Dana woke up with Chloe snuggled against her. They were both still naked. The feel of Chloe's warm body in her arms was exquisite. She breathed her in as she slept. Subtle traces of Chloe's perfume enveloped her senses as she closed her eyes and reminisced.

Making love with this woman was mind-blowingly amazing. She'd always assumed being intimate with someone after Gabbi would feel strange, awkward—that it would take time to adjust to a new partner's body. Being with Chloe was far from awkward. It felt like she'd known her forever and had been waiting for this moment her whole life.

Dana had half expected to wake up feeling like she'd just cheated on Gabbi and was surprised to discover she didn't feel that way at all. She felt just the opposite—like Gabbi would want her to love Chloe in her absence. Especially after what Chloe had been through. She knew Gabbi well enough to know that was how her mind worked.

She gazed down at her new partner in the dark. Maybe they could squeeze in one more round before dinner. This time, she intended to use only her tongue. She lifted her head to check the time when she remembered there was no clock on the nightstand. Her watch was still in the bathroom, so she had no idea what time it was.

Dana reached for her phone on the nightstand. It wasn't there. Neither was Chloe's.

She remembered seeing them there, side by side, just before her towel came off. She was sure of it. Since she was the one closest to the nightstand, there was no chance Chloe could have reached over without waking her. Even if she did, that wouldn't explain why both phones were gone.

She cast her eyes to where the night-light should have been. It wasn't glowing as it had been earlier. Moonlight snaked in through the blinds enough for her to make out the shapes around her. That's when she noticed their towels were no longer in a pile on the floor. They were now neatly folded on the ottoman. The door to their bedroom was open. She had closed that door and locked it herself before they'd made love.

She hadn't known Charlie very long, but she was confident he would never intrude on their privacy. Her mind quickly eliminated all other likely explanations.

The only one left was Sylvio. Every cop instinct in her body told her he was there.

❖

"Chloe, wake up."

Dana's hand brushed against her cheek as she opened her eyes. Full darkness was already upon them.

Chloe sat up in bed and threw a glance at the nightstand before she remembered—no clock. "What time is it?"

"Six thirty," Dana whispered, pressing the night-light on her watch. "We've been asleep for two hours."

Why hadn't Charlie knocked on the door to wake them? Her stomach growled. Maribel had promised to take them all to dinner. Reaching for her cell to check messages, she felt around on the empty nightstand. Her phone was gone. She was sure she had left it right there beside the bed.

"Mine's gone, too," Dana whispered. "He was here."

Chloe slid open the nightstand drawer and breathed a sigh of relief when her hand closed around the familiar shape of her 9 mm. Why would he take their phones but leave their weapons?

"I already searched the bedroom and bathroom. He's gone." Dana pointed to the closed door. There was a chair wedged under the doorknob.

"Where's Charlie?" she asked, sitting up. "Have you been downstairs yet?"

Dana shook her head. "Didn't want to leave you up here by yourself."

Chloe switched on the bedside lamp. Empty clicks filled the quiet space. Her eyes darted to the night-light in the corner. That was out, too. The only source of light in the room was the moon's glow.

As her eyes skimmed over Dana's body, she realized Dana was fully clothed. She had already dressed in her running gear. Smart. Chloe hurriedly climbed out of bed and did the same. These clothes would allow them both to move freely, unencumbered, for whatever battle lay ahead.

She stood from tying her laces, and their eyes met in the dark. "I love you," she whispered. If things went downhill, she didn't want anything to be left unsaid between them.

Dana kissed her sweetly on the lips. "I love you, too."

She shrugged into her shoulder harness, lifted her gun from the bed, and checked to make sure it was loaded. She reached underneath the bed skirt for an extra cartridge and stuffed it inside the waistband at the small of her back.

Walking into an ambush on the other side of the bedroom door was a very real possibility. With an unspoken gesture, she and Dana moved to the window and quietly pushed it open. Gun at the ready, Dana cautiously looked out and scanned the area. From the handful of times she'd tried to sneak out as a teenager, Chloe knew the shingled roof lay a few feet below and extended out about twelve inches. But they'd have to be careful. Twelve inches didn't leave much room for mistakes.

She holstered her gun and went first. Sitting off to one side, she waited and continued to scan the area as Dana climbed out behind her. Now all they had to do was crawl along the rooftop and drop to the sand a story below.

Dana held up her fingers, silently counting. On three, they both dropped and rolled in opposite directions to break their falls. They were back on their feet in seconds, guns drawn at a dark figure in one corner of the yard.

Chloe waited for her eyes to adjust and blinked in surprise. It was Charlie. He was gagged and bound but still alive. With his prized fishing pole propped up beside him, his arms were hoisted above his head with fishing line. It was cutting into his wrists. Blood dripped down the sides of both arms.

Taz was nowhere to be found. Oh God.

She was fighting back tears when a familiar scent wafted in with the ocean breeze. L'Eau Bleue. Sylvio's signature aroma. She froze, smelling the air like a mouse cornered by a snake.

Sylvio stepped out from the shadows. "How nice that you two beautiful ladies decided to join us."

Dana swung around and pointed her gun square at his chest. "Police," she said calmly. "Get your hands up."

Sylvio looked genuinely offended. "I'll do no such thing. In fact, I'm going to reach into my coat here in just a minute and draw my weapon on *you*. Tell me, Detective Blake, what are you going to do about it?" He smiled. His teeth were a radiant white against the backdrop of night, reminding Chloe of the Cheshire cat.

Dana clicked the safety off. "I'll put a bullet in your head, you son of a bitch."

He licked his lips, his eyes roaming Dana's body with an unconcealed lust that made Chloe feel nauseous. "I was just asking my good friend Charlie if he knows how to make a Bloody Mary."

"Last chance," Dana warned. "Put your hands where I can see them."

Ignoring her, Sylvio lifted a martini glass from the picnic table beside him. "Cheers!" He tipped the glass to his mouth and then smacked his lips together. "I make a damn good Bloody Mary if I do say so myself. I'm not in the habit of sharing my secret ingredient, but I'll make an exception just this once." He reached down and withdrew something from the glass, shielding it in his huge palm. His voice dropped to an ominous timbre. "The most important ingredient, of course, is Mary." Instead of the traditional celery stalk, he held up a single human finger. He inserted it in his mouth and began sucking the bloody stump of its juices.

"You sick bastard," Dana said with trembling hands.

It took Chloe a moment to put two and two together. Oh God, no. Not Maribel.

"She certainly was feisty, that one," he said around a mouthful of finger. "And not easily subdued. She adds an interesting flavor."

Chloe steadied her gun on his crotch. "What did you do to Maribel?"

"She's still alive." He dipped the ghostly white fingertip in his drink and brought it to his mouth once again. "Put your guns down. I'll take you to her."

"The only place you're going is to hell," Dana said. She pulled the trigger before Chloe had the chance to pull it herself.

What should have been a perfect shot center chest had no effect at all. Chloe's first thought was Sylvio must be wearing a vest. But then she realized he hadn't even flinched. The average person would have reeled back from a bullet fired at close range.

Chloe had been shot just six months out of the academy. Although the vest had saved her life, she'd ended up with a fractured rib and a nasty bruise. Sylvio was strong, but he wasn't that strong. At the very least, he should have staggered back a step or two.

The barrel of Dana's 9 mm flashed in the night as she fired a second time. Still no reaction from Sylvio.

Staying true to his word, he reached under his coat and pulled out an odd looking weapon that triggered another memory. It was a tranquilizer gun—the same one he'd used on her two years ago.

She raised her weapon, aimed, and fired once in the chest, once in the stomach, and once at the head of the beast. Out of the corner of her eye, she saw Dana bend down to examine a shell casing. But she already knew what Dana would find.

Sylvio had obviously emptied and reloaded their guns with blanks when he took their phones.

Chloe lowered her weapon. Her heart was beating triple-time. An eerie stillness drifted over them, interrupted only by the sound of crashing waves on the shore.

"They're blanks," Dana whispered. "Get out of here, Chloe. Run."

If she left Dana behind, she knew she'd never see her alive again. She suddenly remembered the extra cartridge. She'd kept it under the bed, not in the nightstand drawer with her gun. If Sylvio hadn't found it, there should still be real bullets inside. Her hands shaking, she reached behind her back into the waistband of her pants.

Sylvio steadied the tranquilizer gun in both hands and aimed at Dana. "Sweet dreams," he said, pulling the trigger. A large dart-like object sailed through the air and embedded itself in Dana's chest.

Chloe ejected the old cartridge and clicked the new one in place as Dana pulled the dart from her body and tossed it aside. She took aim and fired as Sylvio did the same. She felt a sharp pain in her left shoulder. Sylvio grunted a split-second later and held a bloody hand to his thigh. With any luck, the bullet had severed an artery and he'd bleed to death.

She tried to discharge her weapon a second time, but her arms were much too heavy. Whatever the dart had injected into her system was already beginning to take effect. Chloe looked down and saw the dart sticking out from her arm. She dropped to her knees in the sand as Dana went down beside her.

"Nice hit." Dana's words were slurred, her eyes unfocused and watery, as she reached for Chloe's hand.

CHAPTER EIGHTEEN

Chloe winced as her eyelids were forced open. Someone was shining a penlight in her eyes. Was she in a hospital? She groaned and rolled her head to one side to get the light out of her eyes. Her head was pounding. Felt like someone had pried her skull open with a crowbar.

"I've given you an injection to counteract the effects of the sedative. There's some Advil and a glass of water here for your headache."

That voice. She couldn't put a name or face to it, but she knew that voice from somewhere. She opened one eye. Everything was blurry. "Where am I?"

Just then, the smell of him hit her and brought everything back at once like a parade of eighteen-wheelers. She tried to sit up but the restraints on her wrists and ankles held her in place. *This can't be happening. I'm at home in my bed. This is just a bad dream.*

The mattress sagged as he settled on the bed beside her. She opened both eyes but could barely decipher the outline of his hulking form. The good news was she still had her clothes on, which probably meant he hadn't touched her. Yet.

"So beautiful." He ran a calloused hand down the side of her face. "Of all the women I've had, you were always the most beautiful. I find myself in a dilemma." He sighed and stood from the bed.

She blinked repeatedly to clear her vision. Objects swam into focus. The bedroom looked exactly like the one she remembered. Same pinewood furniture. Same Berber carpet. Same beige comforter with matching sheets. Sylvio would not have been stupid enough to take her back to the cabin on Naushon Island—not when it was crawling with cops. No, he'd obviously gone to a great deal of trouble to recreate the identical location. But why?

"Detective Blake rivals your beauty," he went on. "I'm having a hard time deciding who to keep. Maybe I'll just have to keep both of you."

She squeezed her eyes shut. At least that meant Dana was still alive.

"Do you have anything to add to sway me in your favor?" he asked.

She knew what she could say to make him angry—maybe even angry enough to kill her, which is what she preferred over being tortured and held here against her will. But that would mean leaving Dana alone with him. She couldn't bear the thought.

Not trusting herself to speak, she looked up at him and said nothing.

"Take some time to think about it," he said, limping over to the nightstand. A dark crimson stain had already spread across the front of his pants. He caught her staring at it and nodded. "I'll be fine. Thanks for your concern. This just reinforces my belief that girls shouldn't play with guns. You can change my bandage as soon as you're feeling up to it."

He popped the cap off the Advil and tapped a few pills into his giant palm. "Take these like a good girl," he said, pushing them between her lips. "For the headache." He held the glass of water as she lifted her head and took a sip.

He smiled down at her. "I want you in tip-top shape for tonight's performance." He limped across the room and flipped the light switch on his way out, leaving her in total darkness. A series of metallic clicks drifted across the room as he bolted the door from the other side.

She flexed her fingers and toes to restore circulation. The thought of being brutalized again by Sylvio nearly made her go mad. But something even more terrifying occurred to her. He was probably with Dana right now. If he hadn't raped Dana yet, he was going to soon. It was just a matter of time.

She began to sob uncontrollably. All she could do was wait and hope Dana was holding her own.

Dana lay in bed cursing her own stupidity. The headache from whatever was in that dart was vicious, but the guilt she felt was much, much worse. She'd assumed finding Sylvio's lair would set him off balance. Instead, it had made him angrier and more focused. She'd underestimated him…again. She should've known better.

She sat up in bed. Her wrists and ankles were handcuffed and shackled. The dim night-light in the corner allowed her to make out her surroundings. Looked like an exact replica of the bedrooms they'd toured with Maribel earlier in the underground tunnel. Why did Sylvio have such a fixation on keeping everything the same? It was weird. She decided not to waste time trying to figure it out.

The bottom line was she had let her guard down, allowing herself to get sidetracked by her feelings for Chloe. Now Chloe, Maribel, Taz, and Charlie were all paying the price for her carelessness. Regardless of the outcome, she knew she'd never forgive herself.

She feared the worst for Maribel, as Sylvio would have little use for her. The thought of losing her best friend was gut-wrenching. She and Maribel had gone through so much together over the last four years. Facing Gabbi's abduction and murder had forged a bond of friendship tighter and stronger than any she'd ever known. She felt her eyes well up. She only hoped Maribel hadn't suffered at the end.

Taz wouldn't have gone down without a fight. There'd been no sign of him, so she allowed herself to hope. He'd already risked his life for her and Chloe, and she felt eternally grateful to him.

Charlie, on the other hand, was like a father to Chloe. Had Sylvio kept him alive to fulfill his own sick agenda? Would he send Charlie on a fruitless search and rescue mission, only to crush his hopes later when Chloe showed up somewhere half dead? Dana seriously doubted Chloe had it in her to come out of this a second time. Who would?

"Sick bastard," she said aloud. What should she hope for now? For Chloe to be alive? In all likelihood, that would mean she'd be brutalized all over again. Better to wish for a quick and merciful death for both of them. Dana simply couldn't imagine having to go through life without her soul mate now that she'd finally found her.

Chloe must have nodded off. She had no idea what time it was, if it was day or night. Unlike the other bedroom, this one didn't have a hairline crack in the ceiling to give her access to the movement of the sun. The fact that she'd been unconscious didn't help. She had no way of knowing how long she'd been out. Hours? A day? Two days? She decided to push it from her mind. She could drive herself crazy with not knowing.

She needed to focus on the things she could control right now: her thoughts, her feelings, even her level of awareness. She could shut everything out, go on autopilot, and hide somewhere deep inside her mind. She'd done it before when things got bad. She knew she could do it again.

Her head snapped up at a sound on the other side of the door. The locks were being disengaged. She closed her eyes and focused. *Click-thump. Click-thump. Click-thump.* There were three dead bolts. Determined not to shed a single tear in his presence, she took a deep breath and steadied herself for what was to come.

Sylvio opened the door and turned on the light. She squinted, blinking furiously to let her eyes adjust to the sudden onslaught of light. Her headache had finally diminished, but she'd been cast in total darkness for what felt like an eternity.

"Rise and shine! I brought you a visitor."

Sylvio was looming in front of her by the time she managed to fully open her eyes. He grinned and stepped aside to let her see who was standing behind him.

Her heart dive-bombed to her stomach. Dana was handcuffed and shackled, wearing the same black Nike running pants and gray top. Chloe scanned her wrists, arms, neck, and face. She appeared unscathed. Dana would have resisted, hard, which probably meant Sylvio hadn't touched her yet. Relief washed over her as they locked eyes.

Sylvio walked to the closet and withdrew two thick metal rings that resembled steel-plated dog collars. He stepped behind Dana, fitted one around her neck, and then moved on to Chloe.

His hand brushed against the side of her face. She winced as he clicked the collar in place. The collar was snug, but it left her with enough room to swallow and move her head from side to side.

He unclipped a long wire lead from the wall and pulled it over to where Dana was standing. He attached it to a small O-ring at the base of her collar, repeating the process with Chloe's.

He withdrew a key from his pocket and unlocked the leather restraints around Chloe's wrists and ankles. She sat up, massaging her wrists. Her fingers were frozen from lack of circulation. She watched as he went to the wall, pulled out a long wire lead until it stopped, and then let it go. It slowly retracted into the wall.

He had them on a retractable leash, she thought to herself.

"This wire can withstand five thousand pounds of pressure. It extends to a maximum length of fifty feet. You can walk around, take a shower, and use the bathroom as you wish. The clip that attaches the wire to each of your collars is locked. I have the only key. Before you get any ideas, you should both know I'll never have the key on me. I've already hidden it in a safe deposit box far from here."

He began pacing the room. "Let's say you decide to strangle me with this wire." He grabbed hold of the wire and wrapped it around Dana's neck to demonstrate. "Keep in mind, your leash does not extend past that door. You won't be able to cut through the wire, not even with a chainsaw. I speak from experience because I've already tried.

"You also won't be able to unlock the steel-reinforced clip from your collar because you don't have the key. I do." He released Dana from his grip. "Good luck getting those collars over your heads because that'll never happen. Even if you succeed in killing me, you'll both starve to death down here. Trust me, no one will ever find you in time."

He stopped pacing long enough to smile at each of them. "The bottom line is, you're mine. I own you until I decide I'm done with you." He strode over to Dana, unlocked her cuffs and shackles, and stepped back, still smiling. "Okay. Any questions, ladies?"

"Yeah," Dana said. "Where's Maribel?"

"Funny you should ask because she was just asking about the two of you. She's next door. Don't have much use for her, though." He frowned. "She's not my type. But she might come in handy when it comes to getting you two to cooperate and do things you otherwise wouldn't."

He sat on the edge of the bed and whispered, "From what I hear, you two have quite the chemistry. I never would've pegged you as a lesbian, Chloe. I realize it was probably difficult for you to fathom being with another man after the heights I took you to." He stood and unzipped his slacks. "It'd be difficult, if not impossible, to find a man who could measure up to this."

Was he going to do this here? Now? In front of Dana?

"Don't you *dare* touch her," Dana spat, stepping in front of him.

Sylvio towered over Dana. At six five, he was easily three hundred pounds and nothing but solid muscle.

"Chloe already knows how this works," he said, never taking his eyes from Dana's. "I say *jump*. You ask *how high*. The word *no* isn't an option here. Saying it only pisses me off."

Chloe watched the altercation between them with a growing sense of dread. She knew the grim reality of the situation. There was no chance she and Dana were getting out of this unharmed.

Dana didn't back down. "There's no way in hell I'm letting you touch her, you son of a bitch."

Chloe leaped up from the bed to come to Dana's defense, but it was too late. Sylvio was already backhanding Dana across the face hard enough to lift her feet from the ground.

Suddenly, he was looming in front of Chloe with that sickening hunger in his eyes. He shoved her to the bed. *Oh God, how can this be happening again?* She didn't bother fighting him off. That always made it worse in the end.

"Get away from her!" Dana shouted, rising to her feet. She grabbed one of Sylvio's muscular arms and wrenched it behind his back.

He straightened to his full height and spun around, breaking free of Dana's hold without even trying. "Don't tell me I can't touch her," he growled. "I *own* her."

"You've already had Chloe. You haven't had me yet." Dana stared at his penis and raised an eyebrow. "You afraid that little guy can't handle me?"

Sylvio reached out, clamped a massive hand around Dana's neck, and pulled her to within an inch of his face. "I believe you're trying to bait me, Detective Blake." His smirk broadened to a grin.

"My last dildo was bigger," Dana retorted with a grin of her own. "Frankly, I'm a little disappointed."

Chloe watched as Sylvio's face turned red. Dana appeared to be the one in control here, and Chloe could tell he didn't like that one bit. He shoved her aside, stormed from the room, and slammed the door shut behind him.

❖

Rubbing her neck, Dana sat on the bed beside her. "Did he—"

"No." They stared at one other, not saying a word. The right side of Dana's face was already beginning to swell. She looked past that and drew strength from Dana's dark, steady gaze. A new worry crept to the forefront of her mind. "He'll make you pay for that."

Dana nodded. "Whatever happens, I need you to follow my lead."

"Not if it means you getting hurt—"

"Listen," Dana said, taking her hand. "You and I both know that's inevitable. We need to deal with the facts right now. We're both going to get hurt. The question is, how much?"

She didn't understand what Dana was asking. Hadn't Sylvio just explained it was pointless to try to escape? It wasn't like they had a choice.

Chloe thought about that for a moment. The one choice they had...sucked. True. But they did have a choice. There were moments in life when having a choice was all that mattered.

She met Dana's eyes and knew they were on the same page. They could either be brutalized repeatedly, or kill Sylvio and risk never being found.

"Your call," Dana whispered. "How do you want things to go down?"

She didn't have to think too hard about that one. "Do you remember the Williams case?" Neither she nor Dana had worked that case, but it had been all over the news.

Dana nodded slowly.

She waited, letting Dana absorb the meaning behind those words.

Nate Williams had returned home early from work as an intruder was stabbing his wife. He'd heard his wife's cries for help, fled up the stairs, and strangled the guy from behind with chicken wire.

"Copy that." Dana squeezed her hand. "We have a plan."

CHAPTER NINETEEN

Chloe shifted on the bed to get closer to Dana. Her stomach growled, but she didn't feel hungry at all. Her internal clock told her they were marching steadily toward the dreaded evening hours, when Sylvio always expected to be serviced.

"He'll be here soon," she whispered. She propped herself up on one elbow and looked where she imagined Dana's eyes were. Total darkness enveloped the room.

"I'm ready." Dana kissed her lips sweetly in the dark. "Whatever happens, Chloe, I don't regret—"

"Shh. Don't talk like that. We're about to kick ass," Chloe whispered. "This is where we hear the theme from *Rocky* in our heads, not *The Sound of Music*."

Dana laughed. "My bad."

It felt good to hear Dana's laugh. She leaned down and found Dana's lips again. Still soft. Still gentle. Still so enticing.

They both jumped as all three dead bolts disengaged, one right after another. She felt Dana's body tense. "Showtime," Dana whispered, sitting up.

The doorknob turned, and the door popped open. Silence. "Dana? Chloe? You guys in here?"

Chloe sat up. "Maribel?"

"Yeah. You two okay?"

"We're fine," Dana said.

Chloe heard a soft whimper across the room, followed by the feel of a cold wet nose on her arm seconds later. "Taz?" She reached out to hug him as he attacked her with a frenzy of kisses and squeals of delight. She felt along his body from head to tail in the darkness. Other than the swollen lip from his earlier run-in with the crab, there were no injuries as far as she could tell. Sylvio had probably darted him with the same tranquilizer he'd used on her and Dana. Her thoughts immediately drifted to Charlie. She had no way of knowing if he was still alive.

Taz led them to Maribel in the dark. "How'd you get in here?" Chloe asked.

"Long story." Maribel reached out and hugged them both. "I can't see shit. Stay still so I can get to the locks on your collars."

"Chloe first," Dana said.

Chloe started to protest but was cut off as cold fingers felt their way around her neck. "Was Taz with you this whole time?"

"No. I was looking for you two and found him first."

"How the hell did you escape?" Dana asked.

"Used to sneak out of the house to see my boyfriend in high school," Maribel explained. "My parents put bars on the windows and locked my bedroom door at night when they found out I was doing the wild thing. I got pretty good at picking locks. It's not something I've ever been proud of." *Click.* "Until now."

Chloe felt the collar loosen. She pulled it off the rest of the way. "You're up, Dana."

"Did he hurt you?" Dana asked.

"Nope. He said I wasn't his type. Said it was my loud mouth that turned him off. Imagine that."

Chloe thought about the finger in Sylvio's drink. "But your hand…"

"Nothing wrong with my hand."

She described Sylvio's macabre cocktail.

"All my digits are intact last I checked. He's torturing someone else." *Click.*

The nurse who recently went missing sprang to Chloe's mind.

"Okay, let's move," Dana said. Chloe felt a hand grasp hers in the dark. "Hold on to each other, and don't let go." Dana led them through the doorway and paused. "We have a choice," she whispered. "Left or right?"

Chloe squinted. Blinding darkness in all directions. It was also freezing. If she could see, she was certain her breath would drift from her mouth like exhaust from a tailpipe on a wintry day. They were obviously in another underground tunnel. How many women had he abducted, tortured, and murdered here? How many lairs did Sylvio have? She shuddered. Maybe they would never know.

She heard Taz's claws as they ticked along the tunnel floor.

"Left," Dana said, picking up on the cue. She tugged on Chloe's hand. "Follow Taz."

Chloe strained to see something…anything. The total blackness was disorienting. They walked single file for two hundred yards or more and finally came to a set of concrete stairs. A small sliver of light snaked along the edges of the door at the top.

"Well, he's nothing if not consistent," Maribel said. "Looks like he put us in the damn basement."

"But he didn't bother with a second security door like he had in the cabin. Why?" Chloe wondered aloud, bothered by how easy this seemed all of a sudden. Was it a trap?

"He trusted the collars," Dana said.

But she knew it wasn't like Sylvio to be so careless.

"Stay here. I'll go." Dana released her hand. "Taz stays behind with you. He's our secret weapon if the shit hits the fan."

Maribel covered Chloe's mouth with one hand as she started to object. "Just let her go first," she whispered. "You two can fight it out later."

Chloe heard the doorknob turn up above. Light flooded the dark space. Dana motioned for them to stay put, silently stepped over the threshold, and vanished from sight.

❖

There was no way she was letting Dana face that psycho alone. She broke free from Maribel's hold and fled up the stairs two at a time.

With Taz close behind her, Chloe nudged the door open wider and stepped into a well-stocked pantry. It looked just like the cabin's pantry. She glanced back down the stairs. Halfway to the top, Maribel motioned for her to keep going.

She scanned the pantry shelves for a knife, scissors, box cutter—anything—but found only rows and rows of neatly stacked canned goods. A metal box on the shelf caught her eye.

This would be too easy, Chloe thought, reaching up. She quietly slid the box from the shelf and popped it open. Inside was a Glock 29 pistol with a second cartridge. She lifted the gun and checked to make sure it was loaded. Satisfied they were real bullets this time and not blanks, she stuffed the cartridge in her waistband.

She found it ironic that Sylvio had chastised her two years ago for not properly storing her gun in a lockbox.

Maribel came up behind her. Her eyes widened when she saw the gun.

Why hadn't Dana come back for them yet? Chloe turned toward the door and listened. Not a sound.

She looked at Maribel. *Wait here*, she mouthed.

Maribel nodded, stepping back.

Chloe gestured at Taz to stay. She inched the door open until she could see part of an unfinished kitchen. Blueprints were spread out on the kitchen counter. No wonder he didn't have tighter security downstairs. This lair was still under construction. Sylvio must have been desperate. He'd obviously had no other place to take them.

She took a deep breath. Gun at the ready, she stepped across the threshold and swung to the right, horrified to see Sylvio standing about fifteen feet away. He had a gun of his own pressed against Dana's ribs. He was using her as a shield.

"Drop it," he hissed. "Or she dies."

Chloe's mind reeled. She couldn't bear to watch the woman she loved get shot to death in front of her. She'd never forgive herself. On the other hand, she knew they were all as good as dead if she complied with his demands.

Warm tears spilled down her cheeks. The muscles in her neck and arms ached with tension as she stood there, gun at the ready, frozen. Dana caught her eye and mouthed, *On three.* Chloe gave a slight nod and pretended to lower her weapon as Dana counted silently on the fingers of one hand. Before she reached three, Chloe gave Taz the hand signal to attack.

Everything happened at once. Dana lifted both feet and dropped to the floor like deadweight. Thrown off balance, Sylvio faltered as Taz bounded around the corner in a blaze of fury. Sylvio raised his weapon and managed to squeeze off a round before Taz reached him. The smell of gunpowder filled the room.

Sylvio screamed in surprise as the German shepherd clamped powerful jaws around his forearm. He shook his head violently back and forth, forcing Sylvio's fingers to unfurl as he dropped the gun.

Taz released his forearm but came at Sylvio again and again. He skillfully dodged Sylvio's blows, tearing large chunks of skin and muscle with each bite. Chloe finally called off the attack, and Taz backed down immediately.

Holding the wounds on his arms, Sylvio staggered. He lowered himself into a black leather armchair, his eyes on Chloe the whole time.

She stepped closer, kicked his gun aside, and stood over him with the Glock. A flash of panic crossed his face. He managed to stifle it with a smile that grazed just the corners of his mouth.

"This is for all the women you've hurt," she said, the tears still wet on her cheeks. She shot one round directly into his crotch.

Wails of agony—along with expletives Chloe had never heard before—filled the small house as he doubled over and tumbled to the floor. He writhed on the carpet for several long and satisfying seconds before he finally grew very still.

Dana joined her. They both stared down at him.

"Is he dead?" Maribel whispered, peeking around the corner.

"Just passed out," Chloe said calmly. She could see his breathing was steady.

As if expecting Sylvio to rear up suddenly, Maribel stood behind them and peered down at him between their shoulders. "I don't think anyone would object if you shot him in the balls a second time," she said. "Or a third," she added. "By mistake, of course."

Chloe considered emptying the cartridge into his crotch but thought better of it. "The offer's tempting, but he'd bleed out. We need him alive for the trial," she said, finally lowering the Glock. "Where's Taz?" She glanced around the room. He was lying on his side against the wall, panting heavily. "Taz?"

He didn't even lift his head. Chloe ran to him and fell to her knees. He'd been shot in the chest. The beige carpet around him was now a darkening shade of crimson. She applied pressure to the wound as blood seeped through her fingers. "You saved us," she told him. "All of us. You're a real-life hero, Taz."

Dana ran over with a towel from the kitchen, handed it to Chloe, and knelt beside them.

"You have to stick around for the award ceremony," Chloe said, holding the towel against his chest. "The chief will give you a medal of honor."

"We'll even invite that ass-head handler of yours," Dana said.

"And he'll have to salute you," Chloe added with a quivering chin. She leaned over until they were nose to nose. "I love you, Taz." She had felt it from the very first day they were together, but she had never said it aloud.

He looked into her eyes, wagged his tail, and kissed her on the chin.

Her head spun around at the sound of a chopper overhead. As Maribel unlocked the front door, she was greeted with shouted warnings from about a dozen uniformed officers. From where she was sitting, Chloe could see they'd formed a perimeter around the front of the house with guns drawn.

"Don't shoot!" Maribel shouted back. She held up her arms as a blinding spotlight illuminated the house's interior.

With her hands raised high above her head, Dana carefully made her way to stand beside Maribel. "Detective Dana Blake. Boston PD. The suspect has been shot. He's down and unarmed. You're clear to enter."

Still pressing the towel against Taz, Chloe heard Charlie's voice as he shouted something to the officers outside. She let out a sigh of relief. Thank God, Charlie was alive.

He was the first to set foot inside the house. He spotted Chloe, ran over, and took a knee beside them. "Good to see you, Cagney."

"Taz took the bullet that was meant for me," she said. "He saved my life. He saved all of us. None of us would be here without him."

Charlie met her eyes and barked out, "Luxon, get over here!"

A tall officer with a crew cut approached. She didn't recognize him. "Is that Taz?" he asked in the deepest voice Chloe had ever heard. "Hey, guys!" He waved his fellow officers over with a beefy hand. "This is that hero dog."

"He's been shot?" someone asked, bending down. "He's still breathing."

"Get the chopper ready!" someone else shouted. "We'll medevac him to the nearest hospital."

"My cousin's a trauma vet," another officer called out from the sea of uniforms that had gathered around them. "She's not far from here. You can pick her up on the way."

Before Chloe knew it, they were loading Taz on a stretcher as one of the medics inserted an IV in Taz's leg. "Never started a line on a dog before," he said, taping the catheter in place. "But a vein is a vein." A second medic traded positions with her and held the towel securely in place as they rushed Taz to the chopper.

"What about me?" Sylvio asked from his handcuffed position on the floor.

The beast had awoken. Chloe shook her head, suddenly wishing she'd emptied her gun into him like Maribel had suggested.

Sylvio snarled, "You better fly me out of here before that damn dog!"

"You'll address that dog properly from now on," Luxon said. "It's *Officer* Taz. Show a little respect." He set a black boot over Sylvio's crotch and stepped down, putting the bulk of his weight behind it.

Sylvio screamed and writhed in agony.

Charlie helped Chloe to her feet, led her outside, and gave her the long hug she so desperately needed. "Don't worry, Cagney. They'll do everything they can to save Taz."

CHAPTER TWENTY

Despite their objections, Chloe, Dana, and Maribel were taken to the hospital. "Protocol," Charlie said, shrugging. "Just go with it." He met them there and patiently sat in the waiting room while they were examined—primarily for potential secondary reactions to the tranquilizer Sylvio had used to sedate them.

Chloe was treated with Advil for her lingering headache and cleared by the ER doc a short time later. It was two fifteen a.m. by the time they all reconvened in the waiting room.

"Any word on Taz?" Maribel asked, shrugging into her suit jacket.

Charlie shook his head. "Still in surgery. We're heading there now."

"Can I come?" Maribel asked.

They piled into Charlie's black Ford Explorer and drove all the way to Tufts veterinary hospital in North Grafton with lights and sirens. Chloe held Dana's hand the whole way there. No one uttered a word. She guessed they were all still reeling from the night's events and worried about Taz.

As was customary for an officer shot in the line of duty, they were greeted by a sea of blue uniforms in the expansive waiting area at Tufts. Chloe could hardly believe it. The sight brought tears to her eyes. Dozens of Boston cops had made the two-hour trek and were now awaiting word of Taz's prognosis.

Making her way through the crowd, Chloe overheard parts of conversations.

"Hell of a dog..."

"Hope he makes it..."

"Best K-9 BPD ever had..."

"Dirtbag deserves the needle for this..."

She stopped at the check-in desk and identified herself. The room fell silent as all heads turned in her direction.

"They're still in surgery," the receptionist said, standing. "I'll see if I can get an update for you."

Chloe watched as he hurried off down the corridor.

A baby-faced cop walked up beside her. She recognized him from earlier. "My cousin's in there now assisting with the surgery. She's the best of the best," he said proudly. "Taz is in good hands."

Chloe smiled and nodded, feeling genuinely grateful. As she waited for the receptionist to return with an update, she noticed one cop sitting alone in the corner. Everyone else was obviously steering clear of him. He had his elbows on his knees and his head down, so she couldn't see his face. But she had a feeling it was Taz's former handler. She'd never had a chance to meet him face to face.

So this was Detective Stevens's ass-head brother.

She instantly felt herself boil over with anger. If he'd had it his way, Taz would have been euthanized a year ago.

When he looked up, their eyes met. He stood, lifted something from the bench, and started toward her. Tears glistened in his eyes as he handed her a small red cooler. "Goat cheese," he said, getting a little choked up. "I hear it's his favorite."

She accepted the gift and felt her anger melt away. "I'll tell him it's from you." She extended her hand as a gesture of forgiveness on Taz's behalf.

"Jethro Stevens. If there's anything I can do—anything at all—you let me know." With that, he turned and walked out. Fellow officers cleared a path for him, but no one bid him farewell.

Dana sidled up alongside her. "What did ass-head have to say?"

She held up the cooler. "He's attempting to make amends with goat cheese."

Dana shrugged. "Well, it's a start."

The receptionist returned but Chloe wasn't sure what to make of his expression. His eyes darted around the lobby as he walked over. She could tell having so many cops in one room was making him nervous.

The room fell silent once more as everyone closed ranks behind her, anxious for the update on Taz.

"He's out of surgery. The doctor will talk with you soon."

"Well, is he okay?" she asked.

"I—I'm not sure. I'm sorry," he said, his cheeks flushed as he resumed his post at the check-in desk.

"How can you not know? You were just back there!" she yelled, frustrated by the lack of information.

"That's one of our own back there," Dana said in her serious cop voice. "At the very least, we deserve to know if Taz is still alive."

"I honestly have no idea. All the doctor said was she'd be right out to—"

"Cagney," Charlie called out from behind them.

Chloe turned as the doctor approached and introduced herself. She was still in her surgical scrubs, booties, and cap. "Dr. Jules, chief of trauma. Taz is still very much alive."

Chloe heard a collective sigh of relief from the room.

The doctor slid the cap off her head. "I won't sugarcoat this. He's in rough shape. The next forty-eight hours are critical." She went on to explain that the bullet had nicked an artery, which she'd repaired. He'd lost a lot of blood. "But we don't know anything yet. He's in a medically-induced coma to minimize the risk of suture rupture. All we can do now is wait and see."

"I don't want Taz to think we just left him here all alone. Can we stay with him until he wakes up?"

"We don't usually allow that." Dr. Jules's eyes widened as she looked around the lobby. Even more cops had gathered in the last thirty minutes. The waiting area, though large, was now bursting at the seams. More uniforms were milling around outside. "Under the circumstances, I think we can make an exception. We've already put Taz in a private ICU room."

"We can take round-the-clock shifts for the next week," Dana said, turning to Chloe. "Between you, me, and Charlie, we'll make it work."

"And me," Maribel said.

"I'll take a shift," an officer shouted out.

"Me, too," someone else said.

"Sign me up," another voice called out.

Before Chloe knew it, they were passing around a clipboard with a rotating schedule of four-hour shifts for the next seven days. She signed herself up for a shift each afternoon.

Charlie insisted on taking the first two shifts. "You've both been through hell," he said, looking from her to Dana. He held out the keys to his Explorer. "Get some rest and come back at noon. I'll call you if there are any changes with Taz."

Ajay Stevens offered to drive Maribel home. Chloe could tell he had a crush on the ADA and thought they'd make a cute couple. She and Dana decided to take Charlie's advice and get some sleep.

Back at Dana's, they showered and climbed into bed, too exhausted even to eat. Fortunately, Dana's house was no longer an active crime scene. BPD had gathered and processed the evidence, and a professional cleaning and restoration company had already begun repairs.

"Taz'll pull through," Dana said. "He's a fighter."

Chloe only hoped Dana was right. She didn't think their life together would be complete without him.

❖

Seven days and a revolving door of police officers later, she and Dana sat on a blanket beside Taz. They looked on in silence as the doctor injected his IV with medication to counteract the sedative he'd been receiving.

"I just want to prepare you," Dr. Jules said. "It's highly likely Taz sustained brain damage from his injury. He probably won't be the same dog you knew before."

They nodded in unison. Chloe felt her heart break a little at the thought. She and Dana had already talked it over. If Taz did, in fact, have brain damage, they were still committed to giving him the best life possible. He deserved at least that much.

She was surprised at how quickly the meds kicked in as Taz lifted his head. He bobbled around a bit as he tried to right himself. "Hey, Taz. We're here, buddy."

Taz didn't look at her or even acknowledge his name.

"Give him some time to come around," the doctor said, getting up from the floor. "Don't let him make any sudden movements. I'll be right outside if you need anything."

They sat together in silence. "Taz?" Chloe said finally. "Can you hear me?"

He met her eyes, his expression blank.

She decided to keep talking, hoping he'd come around. "You took a bullet for me, Taz. You saved my life," she said, feeling the tears well up. "You've been in the hospital for a week, but you don't remember any of it because you were in a coma. We've been visiting you every day. In fact, a lot of cops have been here. Everyone at the BPD is pulling for you, buddy. No matter how this turns out, I want you to know I'm here for you."

"We're all here for you," Dana added. "Even the ass-head." She stood, went to the door, and held it open as Jethro stepped inside. They'd decided this was as good a test as any to gauge the extent of Taz's brain damage.

He walked in slowly and knelt beside Chloe. "Hey there, pal."

Taz wasted no time in voicing his displeasure at the visit from his former handler. Refusing to give him the courtesy of eye contact, he growled without looking over.

"Brought you something." Taz growled louder and bared his teeth as Jethro set something on the blanket beside him. "Should have given this to you a long time ago, pal. I'm sorry."

Taz looked down at the shiny gold shield inscribed with his name. Sniffing it all over, he looked up at Chloe, ears perked.

"You earned it," she said. She pulled out her badge and flipped open the black leather wallet. "See? It's just like mine."

"Here," Dana said, reaching over. "I got you a holder with a chain so you can wear it around your neck." She clipped the badge to the black leather holder and draped it around him. "Now it's official. You're one of us."

Taz wagged his tail in earnest and regarded his former handler with a scrutinizing gaze.

At the risk of losing a finger, Jethro held out his hand. "Truce?"

The room was silent as Taz stared him down for long seconds. With a soft chuff, he finally extended a paw in return.

The two shook hands. With that one simple gesture, they agreed to let bygones be bygones.

CHAPTER TWENTY-ONE

Taz eventually came home and was every bit the dog Dana remembered. She and Chloe had decided it was best for the three of them to stay together, at least until Taz was fully recovered, which meant spending the holidays at her house. Even if Chloe had wanted to return to the condo, Dana would have done everything in her power to persuade her otherwise. She really enjoyed having them here. They felt like a family already.

They hadn't talked much about their living arrangements. She knew Chloe was planning to begin her search for a house after the holidays. At the very least, future plans were up in the air.

But Dana had a plan. Chloe just didn't know about it yet.

She could hardly believe Christmas Eve was already upon them. Charlie and Maribel were due to arrive any minute. They were spending the night with them to help prepare for tomorrow's gathering. A small army would be joining them for the Christmas Day celebration: their colleagues at the BPD, the medevac team from Taz's rescue, and of course, Dr. Jules, along with some of the other veterinary staff from Tufts. Even Jethro was planning to make an appearance. Fortunately, the house her grandfather had left her was huge and would easily accommodate the crowd.

She stopped to admire the Christmas tree that she, Chloe, and Taz had selected together. They'd had a heck of a time getting it home. They finally gave up trying to get it onto the roof of her

SUV and rented a U-Haul. Only after the tree had warmed up and all of its branches fanned out did they realize what a monster it was. At twenty feet tall, it dwarfed everything else in the house. Three trips to Target for countless lights and decorations later, they'd celebrated their hard-won masterpiece with hot cocoa in front of the fire. They'd made love that night with the scent of pine needles on their skin and hot chocolate on their breath until the blazing logs turned to ashes. Dana hoped they were making their first Christmas memories of many to come.

Hands on hips, she surveyed the house. They'd gone all out on decorating and enjoyed every second of it: wreaths, mistletoe, garland strung with tiny white Christmas lights, nativity scenes, villages that lit up and came to life with heartwarming Christmas carols, a life-size Santa with a plate of cookies to greet guests as they entered. Looking around, she realized there wasn't a single undecorated corner. To make the season complete, there was even a blanket of snow covering the ground outside. A classic New England winter was already under way.

Charlie was the first to arrive. Maribel, as usual, was running behind. He looked around as soon as he stepped inside. "Where's Taz? I'm giving him his gift early." He held up a neatly wrapped box. "Got him a stocking with his name on it. There's a squeaky toy inside," he said excitedly.

Dana smiled. She could only imagine what Charlie would be like with a human grandchild. "He and Chloe are running an errand. They'll be back soon." She took his coat and hung it in the closet. "We need to make this quick."

He raised an eyebrow. "Make what quick?"

"I plan to propose to your daughter tonight. But I'd like your blessing first." There. She'd said it. Her hands grew clammy as Charlie stared holes in her head.

Tears welled up in his eyes. "You called her my daughter."

"She is."

He shook his head. "Her real father died when—"

"I know all that," she said, waving a hand dismissively. "You're as much her father as her biological one. Trust me… you're her anchor in this world, Charlie."

He looked down at the floor, silent as he let her words sink in. "Ordinarily, I'd caution you and say you've only known each other a little over a month," he said, finally looking up. "But that's not true, is it?"

Dana grinned as Chloe's nine-year-old face surfaced in her mind.

"I remember how well the two of you got along back then," he went on. "Instant best friends." He shook his head in wonder. "I'm just glad you found each other again. Every father should be so lucky to get a daughter-in-law like you, Dee. Of course you can have my blessing." He opened his arms and gathered her in for a bear hug. "Let's just drop the in-law part and call you my daughter," he whispered.

Before Dana knew it, she was crying, too.

Maribel arrived shortly after Chloe and Taz returned home. "Ajay offered to help if we need an extra pair of hands," Maribel announced, peeling the potatoes.

Chloe slid a tray of gingerbread cookies in the oven. "Ajay?"

Dana had assigned Chloe to baking duty, which was far safer for guests than having her participate in the actual meal prep. Her soon-to-be-fiancée was a lousy cook, but she sure looked cute in her new apron.

"You know…Stevens," Maribel said nonchalantly. "From computer crimes."

Dana added the nutmeg to her famous butternut squash casserole. "Are you two a thing?" she asked as she and Chloe exchanged a glance.

"We are. I think he's a keeper. He has that misleading bad-boy exterior. But he's honest, patient, kind, and responsible." Maribel set the peeler down, turned, and leaned against the counter. "He's smart, too," she said, laughing. "*That* was a nice surprise."

"Cops can't be smart?" Charlie sounded rightfully offended from his corner of the kitchen where he was busy at work on some spinach artichoke dip.

Dana spoke up in her best friend's defense. "Maribel has had a habit of picking bad boys with below-average intelligence since…well…since before I even met her."

"Since preschool," Maribel admitted. "It's been my lifelong affliction."

"Then call Stevens, and tell him to get his ass over here," Charlie said. "It's all hands on deck right now."

By the time Dana and Chloe bid good night to their guests, it was approaching midnight. Working in the kitchen on Christmas Eve alongside the people they cared about most was fun, but it left them both smelling like tomorrow's dinner. They took turns in the shower and met for a long, lingering kiss in the bathroom doorway. Dana had made sure Chloe was the last to shower. She'd needed that time to get things ready.

"There's something I'd like to give you tonight," she said, leading Chloe to the bed.

"I bet there is," Chloe whispered, teasing Dana with a nibble on her ear. "But not if I can give it to you first."

"Are you ready?"

"When am I ever not ready? I could make love to you every night for the rest of my life, and it still wouldn't be enough."

She caught Taz's eye across the room and nodded. He pranced over to them and nudged Chloe's hand with his muzzle.

Chloe looked down. "Well, don't you look handsome."

Taz was wearing the red bowtie that he and Dana had picked out last week. He carefully deposited a gold heart-shaped box into Chloe's palm, just like they'd practiced.

Chloe sat on the edge of the bed and looked up at Dana. "What's this?"

With Taz by her side for support, Dana got down on one knee. She withdrew the box from Chloe's hand and flipped it open. "Will you marry me?"

CHAPTER TWENTY-TWO

Chloe glanced down at her engagement ring as she finished the last of her testimony. Having it there on her finger reminded her how lucky she was to have found the love of her life. Nothing—not even recounting the horrors she'd faced at the hands of a psychopath—could take that away.

It had taken her four days to testify to the abuses she'd suffered over the course of twenty-five days. During that time, she met the jury's eyes without shame. More importantly, she met Sylvio's eyes without fear.

Her captain had referred her to a therapist to be cleared before returning to work. She remembered dragging her feet to that first appointment, determined to expedite the process by saying whatever was needed to return to duty. She didn't see the point in stirring everything up and making herself feel miserable. She was getting ready to start a new life with Dana. She was happy for the first time in a long time. Why couldn't she just focus on that and live fully in the present?

Dr. Levinson had convinced her otherwise. That had been four months and sixteen sessions ago. Now, the shame, guilt, fear, and panic—once so raw and visceral—failed to swim to the surface as she recounted everything from beginning to end. For the first time in two years, she felt like she was finally back in the driver's seat of her life.

She stepped down from the witness stand and strode confidently past Sylvio on her way out the courtroom doors. It felt good to be done with him once and for all.

Dana and Charlie both stood from the bench in the lobby. Taz saw her approaching and welcomed her with a wagging tail and his signature smile.

"You're done already?" Charlie glanced at his watch. "It's only eleven thirty."

She nodded. "They'll probably break for lunch soon."

Charlie looked from Chloe to Dana. "Burritos all around?" He was addicted. Dana had gotten him hooked on her favorite burrito cart outside the courthouse. "My treat," he said to sweeten the pot.

Maribel exited the courtroom and joined them a few minutes later. Dana and Charlie hurried outside to beat the crowd to the burrito man. She and Taz followed Maribel to a private room.

"You kicked ass in there," Maribel said, setting her briefcase in one of the chairs. "As expected, the defense has no witnesses, so closing arguments begin after lunch."

Chloe refrained from taking a seat. "Do you want some privacy to review your notes?"

"Are you kidding? I can recite this closing in my sleep. It's a slam-dunk case. Everyone in there knows he's guilty. Did you see the jurors' faces when you were testifying?"

Chloe nodded.

"With a little luck, they'll reach a verdict quickly, and we'll have something to celebrate soon." Maribel slipped out of her blazer, hung it on the back of her chair, and neatly rolled up the sleeves of her blouse. "Where's my burrito?"

❖

"What if we get caught?" Chloe whispered. She wasn't much of a rule breaker.

"You're just thinking of this now?" Dana whispered back.

"I've been staking this house out for weeks." Charlie glanced at his watch. "We won't get caught."

It was one forty-five a.m. Decked out in black from head to toe, she, Dana, Charlie, Maribel, Ajay, and Jethro looked like cat burglars. Even their faces were camouflaged to blend in with the night. It was hard to tell who was who.

Maribel spoke up from the shadows. "I can't believe I let you crazy people talk me into this."

"Who are you kidding?" Jethro called out. "We all know you would've made a name for yourself as a professional thief if you hadn't gone to law school," he said, referencing Maribel's aptitude for picking locks and sneaking around in the dark.

They all mumbled in agreement.

Chloe gazed longingly toward Sylvio's main residence on Martha's Vineyard. A pale gray contemporary with an abundance of large windows, it sat majestically on the beach overlooking the water. Rather than drive here, they'd navigated around the island, through the Vineyard Sound, and docked at Lagoon Pond in Charlie's boat. They'd walked the pier, scaled the property's short rock wall, and were now hiding behind some bushes. An electronic security gate barred entry from the front, so it had made more sense to approach from the rear.

This house could hold answers to the questions still swimming around in her mind. She knew everyone here wanted to know what made Sylvio do what he did. Realizing she couldn't go through the rest of her life without knowing, she sighed and nodded at Charlie.

One by one, they hunkered down and followed Charlie's lead across the backyard. Taz, of course, remained by Chloe's side the entire way. They climbed the porch steps, pressed their bodies against the house, and held their breath, waiting.

Ajay had already disabled the cameras from afar. Now he carefully examined the keypad to the right of the door. He unzipped his backpack, pulled out a small laptop, and started typing on the keyboard with surprising speed.

Chloe kept her eyes on the keypad and watched as the red light turned green. She heard the lock disengage and let out her breath. No alarms went off.

"Don't look so nervous," Jethro said, reaching for the doorknob. "We got this." He held the door open, and they all ducked inside.

"Remember what we talked about," Dana reminded them in the dark. "Stick to your assigned rooms, take photos of all personal items, and move quickly." She handed each of them a tiny camera attached to a cord that they could wear around their neck.

"The cameras are connected wirelessly to my laptop," Ajay explained, flipping the laptop open to set it down on a nearby table. "Every photo you take will instantly upload. Once a photo uploads successfully, the camera will digitally erase it to make room for the next photo. So don't be alarmed when you see the word *deleted* flash across the camera's screen. I programmed it that way." He slid the cord over his head and looked down. "These cameras are small but mighty. They have a fifty megapixel resolution. We'll get amazing detail when we look at the photos later."

Maribel leaned over to kiss him. "You're such a nerd."

Grinning, Ajay opened his hand to reveal five tiny earbuds. "This is how we'll stay in contact." He held his hand out so everyone could take one. "These earbuds are paired with my phone. I altered the code so they'll transmit to a maximum distance of five hundred yards."

"What happens if we go beyond that?" Maribel asked. "This house is huge."

Ajay shrugged. "Then you'll be out of range."

"What if we trip a silent alarm?" Chloe wondered aloud. "How will we know?"

"We won't," Ajay answered. "That's kind of the point of a silent alarm."

"Which is why we're meeting back here in ten minutes," Charlie interjected. "Tisbury PD will be the ones to respond to the call. They know this house belongs to Sylvio, so they won't be in any rush to get here. Ten minutes should give us plenty of time to get what we need and get out of here before they even set foot on the property." Charlie turned to Ajay. "Flashlights?"

"I thought you brought them."

Everyone froze.

"Kidding," Ajay said, reaching into his bag of tricks once again. He handed everyone a flashlight. "These have specialized low-light beams, so they can't be seen from outside."

"It's a good thing you're on our side of the law," Chloe said, impressed. "You and Maribel could pull off a jewel heist with no problem."

"Speaking of which…" Jethro reached into his pants pockets. "Anyone allergic to latex?" He pulled out six pairs of gloves and passed them around. "No fingerprints left behind."

"Black latex to go with our outfits," Maribel said. "Nice touch."

Locking eyes in the dark, they all synchronized watches. They bid one another good luck, clicked on their flashlights, and expertly dispersed. Charlie had obtained the blueprints online weeks ago, so they already had a pretty good feel for the layout of the house.

Chloe hurried up the stairs to the master suite. Subtle wisps of L'Eau Bleue greeted her as soon as she stepped through the doorway. Taz growled loudly behind her, clamped down on the back of her shirt with powerful jaws, and pulled her back into the hallway. He obviously associated the scent with Sylvio and didn't want her to go any farther.

"It's okay, boy." She turned and knelt down beside him. "The bad guy's not here anymore. He's in jail now. We're safe."

Seemingly satisfied with the explanation, Taz licked her chin and allowed her to proceed.

She made her way to Sylvio's walk-in closet and looked around. All of his clothes were neatly folded and compulsively organized. Versace button-down shirts hung from velvet-covered hangers that were spaced precisely three inches apart on the rod. Searching through the built-in drawers proved less than fruitful—just rows and rows of socks and more tighty-whities than anyone could possibly need in one lifetime. There was nothing of interest here, but she took pictures anyway.

A cursory search of the bedroom and bathroom was just as uninteresting. Turning to leave, she thought about checking underneath the mattress. It was a juvenile place to hide something, but it couldn't hurt to check. She lifted the edges of the mattress and was about to call it quits when her hand grazed the corner of a photo. As she slid the photo out from its hiding place, her arms and legs broke out in goose bumps. A boy of about ten stood alongside an older man. They were holding hands. The man was smiling, but the boy was not.

The boy was obviously Sylvio.

Chloe flipped the photo over. *Uncle Tony—Hyannis, MA* was all that was written across the back. She let out a breath, relieved. This was *exactly* what she was hoping she'd find.

"Team B and E, we have a problem," Maribel's voice came through the earbud loud and clear. "I'm in bedroom three and looking out the window. Tisbury PD just rolled up." She paused. "That's bad, right?"

"Abort mission," Charlie said calmly. "I repeat, abort mission and return to the entry point."

Chloe hadn't had time yet to take pictures of the photo. She couldn't very well steal the photo, so she set it down carefully on the floor and clicked away with the tiny camera. Drawing short nervous breaths, she carefully replaced the photo where she'd found it. She knew Sylvio was never coming back here, but someone would be handling his estate for him at some point. She didn't want to give anyone reason to suspect she'd been here if something went missing.

With Taz beside her, she made her way to the hallway and was halfway down the stairs when she saw a flashlight sweep across the wall in front of her. She ducked down low and crawled down the remaining steps on her hands and knees. When she reached the bottom, she peered around the corner. Everyone was gathered at the entry point. Charlie put his hand up, motioning for her to remain where she was.

"Stay," she whispered to Taz behind her.

She heard a door open a few feet away. "Police," a man's voice she didn't recognize announced. "If anyone's in here, come out now with your hands up."

Taz remained still and mouse-quiet behind her. Her mind reeled. How the hell was she going to get out of this? If they were caught, this could compromise everything. How could she have been so stupid? Everyone's career was on the line now because of her.

Just as she was getting ready to put her arms up in surrender, Jethro sauntered over to the officer. "My bad. It's me you're looking for." Jethro waved behind his back at her to go.

She and Taz stealthily made their way around the corner to join the others. Charlie quietly opened the back door and they all filed out onto the porch, down the steps, and into the dark backyard.

Chloe hid behind a bush and counted the bodies around her. Five of them had made it. The only one who hadn't was Jethro. "We have to go back," she said, trying to catch her breath.

"No we don't." Ajay squatted down beside her. "He said he'd take the fall."

"We can't just leave him here."

"We already did." Ajay pointed toward the water. "And the boat's that way, if I'm not mistaken."

"Cagney's right," Charlie admitted. "He's part of the team. If one goes down, we all go down."

"Haven't you people ever heard of the greater good?" Ajay asked.

"Let's take a vote," Dana suggested. "All in favor of retrieving our fallen comrade?"

Everyone raised their hand, except Ajay. They all stared at him in disbelief.

"What?" Ajay shrugged. "He was mean to me when we were kids." He shook his head and raised his hand reluctantly.

With their fingers laced together and their hands on top of their heads, they trudged single file around the side of the house and into the front yard. They were already standing near the patrol car when two officers emerged from the house with Jethro in handcuffs between them.

"This is a first," one of the officers said.

Charlie cleared his throat. "We're all cops."

"Except for me." Maribel sighed. "I'm an assistant district attorney."

"Good one," the tall officer said. "You're all under arrest for breaking and entering."

Chloe squinted in the darkness at her old partner. "Drew?"

"It's Officer Thomson," he said firmly.

"Drew"—she stepped forward—"it's me, Chloe."

He narrowed his eyes as she slipped the black beanie from her head and shook out her curls.

"Chloe?" A smile broke out over his face, which was instantly followed by a look of confusion. "What the hell are you doing here?"

"This whole thing was my idea," she admitted. "I wanted some answers before they sold the house and took all of his stuff away."

Drew glanced over suspiciously at the group. "That you, Charlie?"

Charlie lowered his hands, removed his beanie, and stepped forward. "Hey, Drew."

Chloe pointed to everyone behind her. As she introduced them, they stepped forward guiltily, one by one. "That's Detective Dana Blake. That's ADA Maribel Murphy. And that's Detective Ajay Stevens. The one in handcuffs is his brother, Sergeant Jethro Stevens. He took the fall for us because he's still trying to make up for flunking Taz here out of K-9 school," she explained, stroking Taz's head as he panted beside her.

"This was a pretty heroic gesture on my part, though," Jethro boasted. "We finally even?"

He frowned as they all shook their heads in unison.

Chloe glanced back at the unlikely group with pride. This moment would almost be comical if their careers weren't on the verge of being flushed down the toilet for good. "Let them go. You can pin this one on me."

Her partners in crime immediately launched a series of protests.

"Take me, instead," Dana said, stepping aside from the group. "I'll go quietly."

"Neither of you is going to jail." Maribel's auburn hair draped around her shoulders as she slipped her hat off and tucked it under one arm. "The upside is I know a lot of lawyers."

"No, no, no." Ajay shook his head. "I was the mastermind behind disabling the security system. Should be me behind bars."

"Don't be silly," Charlie argued. "I'm retired. Makes more sense for me to take the hit on this one."

"But I'm already wearing the cuffs," Jethro said, holding up his hands. "Let them go, and I'll give you a full confession when we get to the station."

Drew remained quiet. He looked down at Taz. "Well? Aren't you going to chime in here?"

Taz lay down and rolled over to expose his belly like a goof, gazing up at Drew in surrender.

Drew sighed and turned to the group. "Did you complete your search of the house?"

They all shook their heads.

"Do you promise not to take anything from the premises?"

They nodded.

"How much more time do you need?" he asked, unlocking Jethro's cuffs.

"Ten minutes ought to do it," Charlie said, smiling.

CHAPTER TWENTY-THREE

With Dana beside her and Taz in the backseat, Chloe drove to Hyannis and parked in front of Anthony Caprazzio's house. "Well, this is it." They all gazed up at the unassuming Colonial.

"How do you want to play this?" Dana asked.

Chloe shrugged. "The truth, I guess."

"Hi, I'm Dana. This is Chloe. We understand Tony Caprazzio kicked the bucket just last week. Are you aware he has a nephew who abducted, tortured, and killed ten women? In fact, he tried to add us to that list, but we escaped and Chloe here shot him in the nuts. We think Tony may have sexually abused him and basically helped to create the sadistic psychopath he is today. Mind if we have a look around?"

"Perfect." Chloe rolled her eyes. "Let's go with that."

Almost as soon as they rang the doorbell, the door flew open. A disheveled middle-aged woman with tired brown hair greeted them with a screaming toddler on her hip.

"You must be the appraisers. Thank God you're early," she shouted over the toddler's wailing. "I'm Grace, the owner's great-granddaughter." She checked her watch as she ushered them inside. "Sorry, I can't stay. Just got a call from my son's school. Couldn't even make it through the first year without breaking his arm." She grabbed her pocketbook off a nearby table and stepped outside. "Take a look around and lock up when you're done. I'll call you later." Without another word, she turned and fled down the stairs to her car.

Dana closed the door and turned to Chloe. "That went way better than I'd imagined."

Chloe nodded. "She did give us permission to look around. Technically, we're not trespassing." They waited for the woman to drive away before retrieving Taz from the car to bring him inside.

They scoured the house from top to bottom in search of anything that would support their theory about Tony. They found nothing that led them to believe Tony was anything but an upstanding guy.

They'd searched every room in the house, including the spider-filled basement. Other than the fact that the house was in desperate need of a thorough cleaning, there was nothing that sent up a red flag. "Maybe the bodies are in the backyard," Chloe said, half kidding, as they ascended the basement stairs.

"It's worth a look." Dana shrugged. "Bet there's a shed back there with some good old-fashioned family secrets hidden inside."

They were poking around outside when Chloe noticed a neighbor peeking through the tall sunflower stalks in her backyard. Chloe smiled and waved.

When the old woman waved back, Chloe walked over to the chain-link fence.

"Morning, dear. I was just weeding the garden," she said, lifting the brim of her straw hat to reveal a wrinkled face with striking blue eyes. "Are you here to sell Tony's house?" she asked.

"We're just looking around," Chloe said honestly as Dana joined them. "Did you know Tony?"

"Oh, my, yes. We were neighbors for sixty years, God rest his soul."

Bingo. Nothing like a nosy neighbor to give you the dirt. "Do you remember a boy by the name of Sylvio?"

Her lips pursed stubbornly as she nodded. "Always trouble, that one. Sylvio came to live with Tony when he was about ten, I think. His mother dropped him off because she couldn't handle him anymore. I remember wondering what kind of a mother could just up and leave her own child like that. But after a few months, I understood why she did what she did."

"What do you mean?" Dana asked.

"I used to see that boy dismembering things in the backyard: insects, frogs, snakes, birds, anything he could get his hands on. And he enjoyed it, too. I could tell from the look on his face. I got me a pair of binoculars and watched him from my living room window." She pointed an arthritic finger at a large window overlooking the yard. "One day, he caught me watching him. I'll never forget the way he looked at me. Evil. Pure evil. The next day, I let my Peaches in the backyard here to do her business, and she never came back. My husband and I looked and looked everywhere, but we never found her. A package showed up on our doorstep a few days later. It was Peaches. Cut to pieces. We knew it was that boy, but we were too afraid to say anything. We had three young daughters of our own at that time, and we were afraid he'd hurt them if we went to the authorities. So we distanced ourselves from Tony and left it alone."

Chloe and Dana exchanged a glance. "Did Tony know what he was dealing with?"

"I think so, yes." She nodded. "He tried everything with that boy. Nothing worked. His mother used to come and visit him every couple of years right before Thanksgiving. After she left, that's when all the neighborhood pets would start to disappear, one by one. My sense was he hated his mother for leaving him." She laughed dryly. "You know what they say…all the problems you have in life can be traced right back to your mother. But I don't think it was her fault. I think that boy was just a bad apple from the beginning," she said. "Faulty wiring, if you ask me."

CHAPTER TWENTY-FOUR

Chloe peered into the nighttime sky. Eighteen months had passed since the trial ended. Sylvio, of course, was found guilty. Chloe slept well at night knowing he would never be a free man again.

It was late September on Martha's Vineyard. Kids had already returned to school, and the beaches were empty once again. The sand under Chloe's feet still held traces of the sun's warmth. With all of their friends, colleagues, and Charlie in attendance, she had married Dana in this very spot on a cloudless day in June. Her hand was still getting used to the gold wedding band on her finger. She'd developed the habit of twirling it round and round with her thumb. It brought her endless comfort to know she had found her other half.

She and Dana had combed the beach earlier for driftwood, which they now added to the growing bonfire. Flecks of charred wood popped and spiraled into the darkness, still ablaze. She stepped back and brushed her hands lightly across her jeans, returning her attention to the task at hand.

There were two piles for sorting: one for frames and one for photos. Chloe unfastened a black metal frame, withdrew the last photo, and handed it to Dana.

She had studied all of Sylvio's victims. Their faces were now safely tucked away in her mind. She promised each of them she would never forget them. A part of them, she knew, would live on through her.

She stood beside Dana, and they both looked down at the photo in Dana's trembling hands. Gabbi stared back at them with a look of heartbreaking despair. Chloe reached out and placed her hands over Dana's to steady them. A full minute ticked by in silence.

"It's time," Chloe whispered, giving her hands a gentle squeeze. "Are you ready?"

Crying, Dana nodded and added Gabbi's photo to the pile.

Maribel had wanted to come and help, but this was something she and Dana needed to do alone.

They sat on Charlie's blue camping chairs and took turns feeding the fire. One by one, Chloe watched as the beautiful faces before her melted into the flames. She recited a quiet prayer, in her heart and on her lips, assuring the women they would never be alone again.

With the last victim freed, Dana wiped the tears from her cheeks and took Chloe's hand. They stared into the fire for long minutes. Chloe was mesmerized by the dancing flames as the fire stole the chill from the air and warmed her body.

"I've been thinking about the house," she said finally. They had put Dana's house on the market just over a week ago and had already received an offer. "I don't think we should sell it."

Dana regarded her as a mix of emotions skimmed across her face. "But we talked about this. You shot two men, and they died in that house—"

"I shot two *sociopaths* who were trying to kill me and abduct you," she corrected. "No big loss to humanity there."

Dana stared into the fire, pensive. "It was also the house Gabbi and I shared together," she said sadly.

"I know. And I've been thinking a lot about that." She scooted her chair closer to Dana's. "Selling the house feels like we're leaving Gabbi behind. If we stay in that house, I'd like to believe a little part of Gabbi is there with us. Since you and she never had the chance to start a family, she should be a part of ours."

Dana was crying again as she leaned in for a passionate kiss filled with promises of more to come later. "Thank you," she said, looking into Chloe's eyes. "You're amazing."

Maribel's voice sounded in the darkness somewhere behind them. "Get a room already."

Chloe could tell from Dana's smile she was happy to see her best friend.

Dana stood to give Maribel a big hug. "What are you doing here?"

"I knew tonight would be hard for you two," Maribel said, leaning over to hug Chloe. "So I brought something to cheer you both up."

"What is it?" Dana asked, frowning.

Chloe laughed out loud. She knew Dana hated surprises.

"Come inside, and I'll show you." Flip-flops dangling from her hand, Maribel turned and started toward Charlie's.

They hurriedly doused the fire with sand, slung the camping chairs over their shoulders, and made their way back to the house.

Maribel was already waiting for them when they stepped inside. "Charlie let me in," she said, fidgeting nervously with a white plastic bag from Walgreens. She was obviously bursting at the seams about something.

Dana nodded at the bag. "What's in there?"

Maribel reached inside and withdrew a pregnancy test. Chloe's eyes widened. "Oh my God! You think you're pregnant?" she asked, feeling the excitement wash over her.

"I'm five days late," she said, opening the box. "I'm never late."

"Wait," Dana said, frowning. "Shouldn't you be doing this with Ajay? He is still your husband, right?"

"Ajay's working tonight. He said it was fine as long as we share the results over FaceTime. By the way, we've already picked you as our future baby's godparents."

"Like that's a big surprise." Dana rolled her eyes.

"We're honored," Chloe said, elbowing Dana in the ribs. "How many tests do you have in there?"

"Four. If it comes back positive, I wanted to be sure."

Chloe looked to Dana and silently asked her permission. Dana nodded.

Before Chloe could say anything, Maribel stared at them, mouth agape. "One of you is pregnant?"

"We're not sure yet," Chloe admitted. "I'm only three days late. We were planning to wait two more days to take the test, but I'll take it with you if you—"

Maribel was already opening the second box and shoving it into Chloe's hand.

"Hey, Taz!" Charlie shouted, rounding the corner. "Time for our movie." He had a huge bowl of popcorn in one hand and a DVD of *K-9* in the other—his favorite police dog movie of all time. His eyes just about fell out of his head when he saw the pregnancy tests.

"So much for trying to be discreet and not get everyone's hopes up," Dana whispered beside her.

She and Dana weren't sharing everything with their friends. She'd been implanted with embryos created from Dana's eggs. If she was pregnant, their child would have Dana's genes but would grow inside Chloe's body.

Chloe's eggs were already frozen, safely stored, and awaiting fertilization from the same donor when the time was right. Dana would carry the second baby with Chloe's egg in a few years.

Well…at least that was the plan, Chloe reminded herself. She took a deep breath. Looked like they were about to find out if their plan had actually worked.

"Will you just take the damn test already?" Charlie asked with a hand over his chest. "I can't take the suspense."

Maribel dashed off to the first floor bathroom. Chloe took the stairs two at a time to use the bathroom on the second floor. They met in the kitchen and set their wands side by side on the paper plate Dana had prepared for them. It was already labeled with their initials, one on each side.

"How long does it take?" Charlie asked, looking over their shoulders.

"Three minutes," Dana said.

"Three of the longest minutes of our lives," Maribel added.

All eyes were glued to the wands. Even Taz was there, sitting perfectly still at Chloe's side.

"I don't see anything." Charlie craned his neck to look closer. "What are we looking for?"

"Two lines means you're pregnant," Dana said.

Just the thought of carrying Dana's baby made Chloe want to cry. It would be the single most important thing she ever did in life.

"This is torture. How long's it been?" Charlie asked.

Dana glanced at her watch. "Two minutes."

"Do you see that?" Maribel pointed to her own wand. Two faint lines were already starting to appear.

Dana and Chloe cheered in unison. They were hugging Maribel in celebration when Charlie suddenly erupted behind them louder than he did on Super Bowl Sunday.

Chloe and Dana looked down at their wand and then at each other with tears in their eyes. They were about to start a new chapter in their lives together.

About the Author

Michelle lives in the Boston area with her two young sons. She garnered material for her stories while working as an EMT, dog trainer, inventor, entrepreneur, and business owner. Her days now consist of changing diapers, chasing a toddler who travels at warp speed, and writing in the wee hours when the kids are asleep—a life she couldn't have dreamed was even possible and wouldn't trade for anything.

Books Available from Bold Strokes Books

A Wish Upon a Star by Jeannie Levig. Erica Cooper has learned to depend on only herself, but when her new neighbor, Leslie Raymond, befriends Erica's special needs daughter, the walls protecting her heart threaten to crumble. (978-1-163555-274-4)

Answering the Call by Ali Vali. Detective Sept Savoie returns to the streets of New Orleans, as do the dead bodies from ritualistic killings, and she does everything in her power to bring them to justice while trying to keep her partner, Keegan Blanchard, safe. (978-1-163555-050-4)

Breaking Down Her Walls by Erin Zak. Could a love worth staying for be the key to breaking down Julia Finch's walls? (978-1-63555-369-7)

Exit Plans for Teenage Freaks by 'Nathan Burgoine. Cole always has a plan—especially for escaping his small-town reputation as "that kid who was kidnapped when he was four"—but when he teleports to a museum, it's time to face facts: it's possible he's a total freak after all. (978-1-163555-098-6)

Flight to the Horizon by Julie Tizard. Airline Captain Kerri Sullivan and flight attendant Janine Case struggle to survive an emergency water landing and overcome dark secrets to give love a chance to fly. (978-1-163555-331-4)

Friends Without Benefits by Dena Blake. When Dex Putman gets the woman she thought she always wanted, she soon wonders if it's really love after all. (978-1-163555-349-9)

Invalid Evidence by Stevie Mikayne. Private Investigator Jil Kidd is called away to investigate a possible killer whale, just when her partner Jess needs her most. (978-1-163555-307-9)

Pursuit of Happiness by Carsen Taite. When attorney Stevie Palmer's client reveals a scandal that could derail Senator Meredith Mitchell's presidential bid, their chance at love may be collateral damage. (978-1-163555-044-3)

Seascape by Karis Walsh. Marine biologist Tess Hansen returns to Washington's isolated northern coast where she struggles to adjust to small-town living while courting an endowment for her orca research center from Brittany James. (978-1-163555-079-5)

Second in Command by VK Powell. Jazz Perry's life is disrupted and her career jeopardized when she becomes personally involved with the case of an abandoned child and the child's competent but strict social worker, Emory Blake. (978-1-163555-185-3)

Taking Chances by Erin McKenzie. When Valerie Cruz and Paige Wellington clash over what's in the best interest of the children in Valerie's care, the children may be the ones who teach them it's worth taking chances for love. (978-1-163555-209-6)

All of Me by Emily Smith. When chief surgical resident Galen Burgess meets her new intern, Rowan Duncan, she may finally discover that doing what you've always done will only give you what you've always had. (978-1-163555-321-5)

As the Crow Flies by Karen F. Williams. Romance seems to be blooming all around, but problems arise when a restless ghost emerges from the ether to roam the dark corners of this haunting tale. (978-1-163555-285-0)

Both Ways by Ileandra Young. SPEAR agent Danika Karson races to protect the city from a supernatural threat and must rely on the woman she's trained to despise: Rayne, an achingly beautiful vampire. (978-1-163555-298-0)

Calendar Girl by Georgia Beers. Forced to work together, Addison Fairchild and Kate Cooper discover that opposites really do attract. (978-1-163555-333-8)

Lovebirds by Lisa Moreau. Two women from different worlds collide in a small California mountain town, each with a mission that doesn't include falling in love. (978-1-163555-213-3)

Media Darling by Fiona Riley. Can Hollywood bad girl Emerson and reluctant celebrity gossip reporter Hayley work together to make each other's dreams come true? Or will Emerson's secrets ruin not one career, but two? (978-1-163555-278-2)

Stroke of Fate by Renee Roman. Can Sean Moore live up to her reputation and save Jade Rivers from the stalker determined to end Jade's career and, ultimately, her life? (978-1-163555-162-4)

The Rise of the Resistance by Jackie D. The soul of America has been lost for almost a century. A few people may be the difference between a phoenix rising to save the masses or permanent destruction. (978-1-163555-259-1)

The Sex Therapist Next Door by Meghan O'Brien. At the intersection of sex and intimacy, anything is possible. Even love. (978-1-163555-296-6)

Unexpected Lightning by Cass Sellars. Lightning strikes once more when Sydney and Parker fight a dangerous stranger who threatens the peace they both desperately want. (978-1-163555-276-8)

Unforgettable by Elle Spencer. When one night changes a lifetime... Two romance novellas from best-selling author Elle Spencer. (978-1-63555-429-8)

Against All Odds by Kris Bryant, Maggie Cummings, M. Ullrich. Peyton and Tory escaped death once, but will they survive when Bradley's determined to make his kill rate one hundred percent? (978-1-163555-193-8)

Autumn's Light by Aurora Rey. Casual hookups aren't supposed to include romantic dinners and meeting the family. Can Mat Pero see beyond the heartbreak that led her to keep her worlds so separate, and will Graham Connor be waiting if she does? (978-1-163555-272-0)

Breaking the Rules by Larkin Rose. When Virginia and Carmen are thrown together by an embarrassing mistake they find out their stubborn determination isn't so heroic after all. (978-1-163555-261-4)

Broad Awakening by Mickey Brent. In the sequel to *Underwater Vibes*, Hélène and Sylvie find ruts in their road to eternal bliss. (978-1-163555-270-6)

Broken Vows by MJ Williamz. Sister Mary Margaret must reconcile her divided heart or risk losing a love that just might be heaven sent. (978-1-163555-022-1)

Flesh and Gold by Ann Aptaker. Havana, 1952, where art thief and smuggler Cantor Gold dodges gangland bullets and mobsters' schemes while she searches Havana' s steamy Red Light district for her kidnapped love. (978-1-163555-153-2)

Isle of Broken Years by Jane Fletcher. Spanish noblewoman Catalina de Valasco is in peril, even before the pirates holding her for ransom sail into seas destined to become known as the Bermuda Triangle. (978-1-163555-175-4)

Love Like This by Melissa Brayden. Hadley Cooper and Spencer Adair set out to take the fashion world by storm. If only they knew their hearts were about to be taken. (978-1-163555-018-4)

Secrets On the Clock by Nicole Disney. Jenna and Danielle love their jobs helping endangered children, but that might not be enough to stop them from breaking the rules by falling in love. (978-1-163555-292-8)

Unexpected Partners by Michelle Larkin. Dr. Chloe Maddox tries desperately to deny her attraction for Detective Dana Blake as they flee from a serial killer who's hunting them both. (978-1-163555-203-4)

A Fighting Chance by T. L. Hayes. Will Lou be able to come to terms with her past to give love a fighting chance? (978-1-163555-257-7)

Chosen by Brey Willows. When the choice is adapt or die, can love save us all? (978-1-163555-110-5)

Death Checks In by David S. Pederson. Despite Heath's promises to Alan to not get involved, Heath can't resist investigating a shopkeeper's murder in Chicago, which dashes their plans for a romantic weekend getaway. (978-1-163555-329-1)

Gnarled Hollow by Charlotte Greene. After they are invited to study a secluded nineteenth-century estate, a former English professor and a group of historians discover that they will have to fight against the unknown if they have any hope of staying alive. (978-1-163555-235-5)

Jacob's Grace by C.P. Rowlands. Captain Tag Becket wants to keep her head down and her past behind her, but her feelings for AJ's second-in-command, Grace Fields, makes keeping secrets next to impossible. (978-1-163555-187-7)

On the Fly by PJ Trebelhorn. Hockey player Courtney Abbott is content with her solitary life until visiting concert violinist Lana Caruso makes her second-guess everything she always thought she wanted. (978-1-163555-255-3)

Passionate Rivals by Radclyffe. Professional rivalry and long-simmering passions create a combustible combination when Emmett McCabe and Sydney Stevens are forced to work together, especially when past attractions won't stay buried. (978-1-163555-231-7)

Proxima Five by Missouri Vaun. When geologist Leah Warren crash-lands on a preindustrial planet and is claimed by its tyrant, Tiago, will clan warrior Keegan's love for Leah give her the strength to defeat him? (978-1-163555-122-8)

Racing Hearts by Dena Blake. When you cross a hot-tempered race car mechanic with a reckless cop, the result can only be spontaneous combustion. (978-1-163555-251-5)

Shadowboxer by Jessica L. Webb. Jordan McAddie is prepared to keep her street kids safe from a dangerous underground protest group, but she isn't prepared for her first love to walk back into her life. (978-1-163555-267-6)

The Tattered Lands by Barbara Ann Wright. As Vandra and Lilani strive to make peace, they slowly fall in love. With mistrust and murder surrounding them, only their faith in each other can keep their plan to save the world from falling apart. (978-1-163555-108-2)

Captive by Donna K. Ford. To escape a human trafficking ring, Greyson Cooper and Olivia Danner become players in a game of deceit and violence. Will their love stand a chance? (978-1-63555-215-7)

Crossing the Line by CF Frizzell. The Mob discovers a nemesis within its ranks, and in the ultimate retaliation, draws Stick McLaughlin from anonymity by threatening everything she holds dear. (978-1-63555-161-7)

Love's Verdict by Carsen Taite. Attorneys Landon Holt and Carly Pachett want the exact same thing: the only open partnership spot at their prestigious criminal defense firm. But will they compromise their careers for love? (978-1-63555-042-9)

Precipice of Doubt by Mardi Alexander & Laurie Eichler. Can Cole Jameson resist her attraction to her boss, veterinarian Jodi Bowman, or will she risk a workplace romance and her heart? (978-1-63555-128-0)

Savage Horizons by CJ Birch. Captain Jordan Kellow's feelings for Lt. Ali Ash have her past and future colliding, setting in motion a series of events that strands her crew in an unknown galaxy thousands of light years from home. (978-1-63555-250-8)

Secrets of the Last Castle by A. Rose Mathieu. When Elizabeth Campbell represents a young man accused of murdering an elderly woman, her investigation leads to an abandoned plantation that reveals many dark Southern secrets. (978-1-63555-240-9)

Take Your Time by VK Powell. A neurotic parrot brings police officer Grace Booker and temporary veterinarian Dr. Dani Wingate together in the tiny town of Pine Cone, but their unexpected attraction keeps the sparks flying. (978-1-63555-130-3)

The Last Seduction by Ronica Black. When you allow true love to elude you once and you desperately regret it, are you brave enough to grab it when it comes around again? (978-1-63555-211-9)

The Shape of You by Georgia Beers. Rebecca McCall doesn't play it safe, but when sexy Spencer Thompson joins her workout class, their non-stop sparring forces her to face her ultimate challenge—a chance at love. (978-1-63555-217-1)